# SPIRITS

**Rachel Huon**

# Contents

# Chapter One

-------------------------------------------------------------

I was in my studio, listening to music as I cleaned up the mess the kids had made during their lesson yesterday. I had started working as an art instructor when this studio was passed down to me by my parents because they decided they wanted to retire and travel the world together.

I had studied for four years for an art degree and as soon as I got it my parents handed me the studio which mom had previously used to teach ballet to young teenagers.

When I was young my mom had tried to teach me how to do ballet but I could never quite grasp the concept and instead always strayed towards my pencils and paint brushes.

When I got the studio I offered classes to kids from 7 to 15 years old and at first it wasn't doing quite well until my older brother recommended it to some of his friends who had kids.

After a year my class was filled with a total of fifteen kids coming twice a week. In my free time I would occasionally go to the elementary school that was on the same street and would volunteer to do art activities there which the principal and school staff were very grateful for.

As I finished up cleaning I looked up at the time and realized that today was Friday, one of the days I would go to the school and it was almost 1 already.

I quickly grabbed my bag and winter jacket since it was quite cold here in Winnipeg and headed out after locking the doors.

The walk to the school was very short and when I walked in and headed to the main office to tell the secretary I was there and asked her which class would attend the activity today.

"Class 031 will be with you in the vacant art room." She told me and I smiled.

I wasn't supposed to have favourites but class 031 was definitely my favourite. Ethan, a little 8 year old boy who was actually one of my students was an absolute angel and no one could resist coddling him, me included.

As I walked in the vacant art room which the school basically called it "Ms Vernon's classroom" I was met with the cheers of the kids.

"Miss Vernon!" They all exclaimed and I smiled.

"Hi guys!" I replied as I set my things down on the desk and gave a small smile to Mr. Ross who was their main teacher.

"Do you guys want to draw or paint?" I asked, already knowing the answer.

"Paint!" They all said and I grinned.

"Alright. You guys know what to do right?" I asked and they all nodded, getting up and going to grab their things to paint.

As I watched over them, making sure no one spilled or broke anything I felt someone staring at me from behind.

I turned to Mr. Ross who looked like he was debating what to do.

"Everything alright?" I asked and he snapped out of it.

"Yes everything is fine." He said with a clear of throat.

"Actually Miss Vernon..." he started off. "There's this work dinner after classes today and some of the other teachers and some more friends of ours will be attending. Do you want to join?"

"When will it be?" I asked politely but to be honest I really did not want to go out tonight.

"At 7. It's at the new restaurant that opened up last week near the mall." He said and suddenly the images of the delicious food that was served at that restaurant flashed in my mind.

I was planning on going with my friend, Carmen but she's been extremely busy so I figured this was my chance to try the food and see if it tastes as good as it looked on their Instagram page.

"You know what? I'll be there." I said and he grinned.

"Miss Vernon!" I heard a whine and I turned to see Ethan pouting.

"Yes sweetheart?" I asked, walking over to where he was sitting.

"I was trying to paint a large flower field but it looks so weird now with the yellow!" He exclaimed pointing over to his canvas.

"Aww it's not that bad! Look let me help fix it." I said and started to help him.

-

I was finally done getting ready for the dinner. I wore a cream coloured sweater and some black jeans since it was cold outside. I grabbed my jacket, bag and phone and then left my small apartment which I lived in alone.

I loved being with my friends and family but I also really treasured my independence and space. Living alone always brought me a sense of peace. Of course sometimes Carmen would come over or I'd go over her house and we'd have our girls night but that was once a month at most.

I had to drive to the restaurant since it was quite far and this was not a good weather to take a walk. The drive was about fifteen minutes and when I arrived it was 7:07

I hope Mr. Ross and some other teachers I knew would already be there as I did not want to walk in and know no one.

Thankfully when I walked in they were already seated at a table in the corner and I noticed there were only five people there.

I walked closer to them and Mr Ross noticed me, he smiled and waved me over.

"I'm glad you made it, Miss Vernon!" He said and then motioned for me to sit across from him and next to a man I had never seen before.

"You can call me Hyacinth." I told him with a small smile, taking off my jacket and sitting down.

As I sat down the man next to me turned to stare at me with a calculating gaze and when I turned around to look at him he smirked.

"Nice to meet you Hyacinth." He emphasized on my name.

"Nice to meet you..?" I trailed off, not knowing his name.

"Roger." He supplied.

Roger was probably tall, because even sitting down I had to arch my neck to meet his dark green eyes. He had blond hair that fell over his forehead and a sharp jawline. His features made him look sweet and cute but the look in his eyes wasn't exactly cute.

As I continued to stare at him and decide wether I should continue the conversation with him or not other people started introducing themselves and so my attention was strayed.

After a couple minutes of chatting the waiter arrived to take our orders.

I ordered the cheesy spaghetti with the garlic bread and soda since I had to drive back.

"You're not going to drink?" Roger asked and I turned to him again.

"No, I drove here." I answered.

"What a shame." He muttered and I nervously smiled.

"Are you also a teacher?" I asked him and he shook his head.

"No I'm just a friend of Ross over there. I actually work at a company called 'Les Papillons.' Have you heard of it?" He asked, taking a sip of his red wine.

"Oh is it the one the one that makes toys?" I asked and he grinned.

"Yeah, I'm in charge of getting the toys where they're supposed to be." He said with an excited glint in his eyes and I internally awed.

We continued to quietly converse between us and I got to know a lot more about him. He had a brother and nephew in Calgary and he loved to visit them. He also loved to go out to hike, go to the forests and run.

He was a very funny and charming man and if I said I wasn't charmed then I would be lying. As the night came to an end he had draped his arm over the back of my chair and we had finished to eat the food that did indeed taste as good as it looked. The rest of the people already left and so we were the only two left in our group.

"It's getting late, I think I'm gonna leave." I said and he groaned in disappointment but nodded, getting up and helping me into my jacket as a light blush coated my cheeks.

"Hyacinth." He said grabbing my wrist after I zipped up my jacket.

"Can I see you again?" He asked, raising his hand and brushing a lock of my hair away from my face.

"Yes." I answered softly and he smiled.

"Give me your number?" He asked, getting his phone out and I typed it in.

"I'll see you soon." He softly uttered then lent down and pressed a kiss to my cheek.

# Chapter Two

"Are you sure this is a good idea?" Carmen asked, from where she was sitting on my bed.

"Why wouldn't it be a good idea?" I retorted while applying a light coat of lipstick on my lips.

I looked at my appearance and smiled in approval. My dark brown hair that fell to my shoulders was straightened and my blush that coated my cheeks was quite visible. I put some eyeliner on my eyes to make them more visible and it really did make my dull brown eyes seem a little brighter. I was wearing a cute black top and jeans with my boots and my white jacket.

"This is the first time in two years that you're going out with a man. And that too, a man you met two days ago." Carmen answered and I shrugged my shoulders.

"I just feel like it's time for me to start dating again, and he was a very nice man." I smiled over my shoulder and she chucked.

"Alright, just be careful." She said and then glanced at my outfit. "Isn't it a bit casual?"

"He said to wear something casual and it's really cold outside today so this will have to do." I replied, running my hand over the soft and warm fabric of my shirt.

"I wish I could call you after to make sure it went alright but I have to drive for the next four hours and after that I'll barely have any connection or even time to contact you." She said with a worried frown.

"Carmen, there's no need to worry about me. I'll be fine." I assured her.

Carmen was a gorgeous dark skinned 25 years old who owns her own hairdressing salon which is very fitting since she has the most stunning hair I have ever seen and she's really good at styling it. She's an absolute angel and we became best friends when I visited her salon three years ago. But Carmen did have the tendency to worry quite a bit about the people she cared about.

Every year during the Christmas holidays she would go and visit her grandma who lived in a small house just outside of the city. Her grandmother did not have any internet connection saying it was unnecessary. She simply had a landline that did not need the internet.

"If something happens, call at my grandma's house, alright?" She said and I nodded in agreement.

"He's going to come pick you up?" She asked looking at the time.

"Yeah he said he'll text me when he's downstairs." I replied, sitting next to her on the bed.

"Are you nervous?" She asked me.

"Not really, I'm not sure how this is gonna go but even if it doesn't end well it won't bother me much since I did just meet him." I answered and she hummed.

My phone buzzed with a notification and I looked at it to see it was Roger saying he was here.

"Alright I'm going now, don't forget to lock the door on your way out." I told Carmen and then I hugged her tightly.

"I'll miss you but have fun with your grandma!" I told her and she laughed.

"I'll miss you too, babe." She hugged me back just as tightly before pushing me to the front door.

I made my way out of my apartment complex before walking to the nearest store where I had told Roger to meet me. I didn't feel comfortable telling him my exact address and he did ask me why at first but then decided to let it go and agreed.

As I walked closer I caught sight of him leaning against his car, wearing a hoodie with his jacket on top and black jeans.

"Hey." I called out when I was close enough and he turned to me.

"Hello, Hyacinth." He smiled, walking over to me and grabbing my hand. "You look wonderful."

"Thank you, so do you." I said with a small blush and he grinned.

He led me to his car and opened the door of the passenger seat and before I could get in he lightly kissed my cheek making me smile in giddiness. He also got in and then he started driving.

"Where are we going?" I asked and he smiled. "I'm not telling you."

"Oh alright." I chucked, I guess I could handle a little surprise.

As we continued going down the road he moved his hand and placed it on my knee, making my stomach flutter and a smile come onto my face.

I glanced at his face and tilted my head, the way he was smiling was different then how he was smiling the other night. It had so much more intent and the small glint in his eyes that seemed like excitement to me could have easily been mistaken for danger.

I broke out of my thoughts when the car slowly came to a stop and I looked out to see we were around a forest.

"Isn't this..." I trailed off and he filled in for me. "Bois-des-Esprits?"

"Yeah! I heard a lot of people stopped going here. Are we allowed?" I asked and he nodded.

"Don't worry, we are." He said and got out of the car as I followed.

He grabbed my hand and started leading me inside and as we walked I could hear the branches and the leaves crunching underneath our boots.

"Are you taking me somewhere to murder me?" I asked jokingly and he laughed, a loud sarcastic laugh.

"Of course not." He answered looking back over his shoulder with the same dark glint in his eyes and suddenly my stomach was no longer fluttering with butterflies but instead squeezing in unease.

"Isn't it a bit cold to go to a forest for our date?" I chuckled nervously as a strong wind started blowing.

"You won't be cold for long." He said, tightening his hold on my hand and walking faster.

I was starting to genuinely feel scared and I wished I had listened to Carmen and thought over going on a date with a man I just met.

But he was friends with Mr.Ross so surely he wouldn't turn out to be a lunatic.

Right?

"Roger, could we go back? I don't feel very good." I lied hoping he would listen but he ignored me and continued walking.

I tried to pull my hand out of his hold but he wouldn't budge.

"Stop!" I yelled but he didn't.

He kept walking and walking as I struggled and dragged my feet on the ground to slow him down.

"Roger, please let me go!" I pleaded but once again my words fell deaf against his ears.

What should I do? What on earth should I do?

As I was panicking he finally stopped walking and turned to me with the same smile.

"Hyacinth, are you quite alright?" He asked and I furrowed my brows in confusion.

"Would you let me go?" I asked tugging my hand but he kept it in his hold, surely bruising it at how tight he was holding it.

"Now just wait a moment, I have to make a call." He said and took out his phone with his other hand.

I stood there in complete confusion on what was going on. Why was he acting so weird? Who was he calling?

He held the phone to his ear and it seemed the other person replied as his eyes brightened.

"I have her." He said and then he listened on what the person was saying.

"Ok." He said and then he cut the call.

"Who was that?" I asked.

"No one." He said.

"Let me go." I said holding his hand with my other hand and tried to pry it away.

It was a bad idea to do so because he suddenly remembered I had two hands and he grabbed hold of the other as well and pushed me back until I hit a tree and he pinned my arms above my head keeping my body pressed against the tree with his.

He was so close and he was staring at me so darky. My heart was hammering inside my chest and I wanted to disappear but I knew I was stuck.

As I continued to struggle against him, my hands scratched against the tree trunk making them sting but I ignored it. Snow started to fall and the wind started to pick up once again making the tree leaves blow and I could hear loud noises as branch thumbed on the ground.

I glanced to my left where a long and thick branch fell and with a last ounce of hope I raised my leg and kneed him as hard as I could.

"Let go!" I yelled and thankfully one of his hands fell from my hand and I hurriedly grabbed the heavy branch and hit him straight on the head making him let go of me completely.

Before he could even think about making his other move I turned and started running as fast as I could.

The snow started falling even more making my vision blurry but I didn't let it stop me. I had to get away.

I had to.

I could hear him catching up to me and I ran faster and faster. As I turned around to see if he was closer my feet caught another fallen branch and I fell.

I didn't notice the small hill that was right in front of me and as I fell I started to roll down the hill and a scream left my lips.

I groaned in pain as my leg hit a rock at the bottom of the tree. I slowly pushed myself up and glanced up the hill to see he wasn't there.

At least not yet.

I looked down at my legs and winced at the sight of my ripped jeans and the blood that was starting to form on my right one.

"It's okay, ignore it." I told myself and started to walk.

Every step I took, a burning pain shot up to my leg but I forced myself to ignore it and moved as fast as I could.

It felt like I was running for hours when it could have only been around 5 minutes.

The more I ran the worse the pain got and I simply wanted to give up and let go but I knew I couldn't.

Not only was the snow blurring my view but so were the tears that felt like ice against my skin. My breathing was ragged and my heart beat was out of control and I really really wanted to give up.

"I c-cant." I whimpered and stopped to lean on a tree. I looked up at my surroundings and my eyes widened when I saw a small cabin a few meters away from me.

Was someone there?

I pushed myself off the tree and forced my legs to move closer to the cabin.

Just a bit more, just a bit more.

I finally reached the door and I immediately banged my hand against the door.

"Is anyone there?" I yelled, continuing to bang and then I heard the doorknob turn and my entire body lost the tension as the door opened and the last thing I saw was a blurry face of a man before my legs gave out.

# Chapter Three

My body gave out but my brain was still wide awake, with panic.

Before I could hit the ground, a strong arm wrapped around my waist and the other held my arm.

"Woah easy there." I heard a gruff voice murmur in confusion before I was getting picked up in his hold and the door shut behind us as he walked in and I savoured the warmth of the cabin.

He gently set me down on a couch and then he left the room leaving me alone, and panicked. My breathing was heavy, my chest was squeezing and my mind felt dizzy.

What just happened?

I could hardly gather my thoughts and my breathing was getting shorter and my lungs were screaming at me.

"Hey hey." I heard the same voice and then my face was being held by big, warm hands that tilted my head upwards.

I still had teary eyes and so I could only make out a blurry face and black hair.

"Breathe, darling, breathe." He whispered as he wiped a fallen tear from the corner of my eye but I couldn't.

I couldn't breathe.

I was hyperventilating.

"You're safe now." He continued to say.

"Just focus on my voice and take a deep breath for me." He pushed and I did.

I took a breath and then he told me to do it again and again until I was breathing normally.

"That's it, you're doing so good." He continued to say in a soft voice as I finally calmed down.

He let go of my face and grabbed a glass of water which I just noticed and helped me drink. I pushed the glass away when I had drank enough and then blinked away the tears to look at his face.

The first thing I noticed about him were his eyes.

They were grey, and they reminded me of clouds before a storm would hit. They were so stunning. He had black hair that was messy but looked very soft. His eyebrows were furrowed in worry and his face was also set in a worried but questioning frown. He had a light stubble and his body was tall and big compared to mine.

His whole body was muscular and he looked like someone who would be a professional boxer.

"Are you alright?" He asked, sitting down next to me and I noticed a hint of a British accent in his voice.

"I-I think so." I answered hoarsely.

"Your leg looks really bad, would you mind if I take a look at it?" He asked cautiously and suddenly the pain in my leg came back full force as I glanced back at it.

My blue jeans were now ripped and wet with blood and when I glanced at my hands they too were covered with scratches from the tree trunk.

"My jeans." I mumbled. How was he gonna take a look at my legs with my jeans like that?

"I can give you some clothes to change into and then I'll look at it, okay?" He suggested and I nodded.

He got up and walked towards a door which I presumed led him into a bedroom. I took the chance to look around and I let a small tired smile come into my face as I glanced at the cute cabin.

It was made out of wood and it was small but seemed to have all the necessities. To the left of the living room there was a small hall which I assume would lead to the kitchen and next to the bedroom door there was another door which was probably a bathroom.

He also had a fireplace and there was actual fire, warming up the cabin. I decided to take off my jacket as it had gotten quite dirty from my fall.

When I glanced at my shirt I was glad that at least once piece of my clothing wasn't ruined. I also decided to take off my boots and socks and when I glanced at the wooden floor under me I immediately felt bad for getting it wet.

"Here you go." He came back with a dark blue shirt and some shorts.

"Thank you." I muttered grabbing the clothes from him.

"I'll be back in my room, call out to me when you're done." He told me and I nodded as he walked back inside and closed the door behind him.

I took off my shirt and bra hoping his shirt would cover me modestly and then slid it on and it felt so soft and loose against my skin making me feel ever more relaxed. It also smelled really good.

Like cinnamon rolls.

My stomach grumbled at the thought of food and I huffed.

I tried to get up to take off the jeans but as soon as I stepped on my injured leg a huge wave of pain hit me and I immediately fell back on the couch with a whimper.

"Shit!" I groaned, closing my eyes and the door from the room immediately opened.

"What's wrong?" He asked walking over to me and kneeling in front of me.

"I-I can't get up." I whispered in embarrassment.

"Oh.." he answered and then looked around as if something would magically appear and help me get up.

"Do you want me to help you?" He asked and I stared at him.

"How?"

"You can lay down and I-I can um take off your pants." He said lowly.

"What?" I asked with wide eyes.

"I know this is really weird and I promise I'm not trying to take advantage of you but you have to get out of these jeans." He told me.

I hesitated.

I did not trust this man and what if I had escaped one lunatic only to meet another one?

But I also knew that I had no one else but this man that can help me and so I would have to give him some blind trust and hope he doesn't end up disappointing me.

And if he wanted to hurt me he could have done it the moment I showed up at his door.

But he didn't. Instead he calmed me down and is offering to clean up my wounds.

"Alright." I nodded, my face flaming in heat.

"Just lay down on the couch." He said softly adjusting the small pillow behind me.

I moved further back on the couch and raised my non-injured leg on it and then he softly grabbed my bloodied one underneath my knee and helped me get it on the couch.

His touch was gentle and somehow reassuring that he wouldn't try to hurt me even more.

I slowly leaned back until my head hit the pillow and I was laying down with my legs flat on the couch making me feel some relief.

"Alright I'm gonna have to raise the shirt a bit." I heard his voice say and when I looked at him I saw him already looking at my face.

I slowly nodded my head and he raised his hand to my shirt, all while keeping his eyes on my face and slowly raised my shirt until the top of my jeans were visible.

I then felt his hand on the button of my jeans as he unbuttoned it, the back of his knuckles brushing against my abdomen making my stomach clench.

"Raise your hips." He murmured, keeping his eyes on mine and I did.

He quickly slid my jeans off and didn't dare glance down which I was extremely grateful for. As soon as the jeans were under my butt I lowered my shirt until it covered my underwear and then lowered my hips back on the couch.

He moved his eyes away from me as soon as I lowered my shirt and then he backed away a bit to get closer to my legs.

"It might hurt a bit when I take it completely off as it's going to rub against your injury." He warned and I nodded, not having the voice to talk.

I closed my eyes in anticipation of the pain and it did not disappoint me. As soon as he took the rest of my jeans off my legs I could feel the area burn and I hissed.

"Sorry, it's almost done." He whispered.

"There you go." He said getting back up and then he told me to stay put before he disappeared once again with the rest of my clothes.

He came back with a first aid kit and kneeled back on the floor.

"That's a really bad gash." He muttered, making me raise my head to look at it.

My eyes widened at the sight of my swollen, bloodied and practically purple leg.

"That is disgusting." I huffed and let my head fall back.

"Don't worry, it'll go away soon." He tried to assure me but we both knew that was going to leave some kind of mark.

"What's your name?" I asked, to distract myself from the acid he was about to apply on my leg.

"Aster." He answered, making me smile.

(A/N: Aster>Roger )

"I like your name." I said as he cleaned around my leg to get rid of the blood. "It's my favourite flower. And the flower's colour is my favourite colour."

"What's yours?" He asked, applying some kind of antibiotic on my injury making me wince.

"Hyacinth." I said in between clenched teeth making his hand freeze for a brief moment.

"Funny enough, that's my favourite plant." He said.

"Really?" I asked in disbelief and he hummed.

"I have a pot of them in my room." He told me as he wrapped a bandage around my legs, his fingers rough but his touch soft against my skin.

He grabbed the black shorts he had brought for me and then he put each leg in before moving it upwards.

"Up." He said and I raised my hips as he pulled them all the way up.

"There you go." He said, grabbing my hands in his much larger ones and pulling me back up to sit.

"Your hands look like they're hurt too." He said, glancing at them and I sighed.

"Yep."

"Do you wanna tell me what happened and what you're doing here?" He asked, sitting down next to me and starting to clean up my hands.

"Can I get food first?" I mumbled as my stomach grumbled again.

"Of course, darling." He said with a small smile, the first one since I arrived and I couldn't help but smile back.

Hello!I hope you guys enjoyed the chapter.

What do you think of Aster?

If it wasn't clear already Roger is not the male lead.

With that said, here's Aster's character aesthetic:

This is a bit how the cabin looks like but for the kitchen instead of green and white I imagine it as black:

Yes there's a bathroom but I couldn't find any good picture :(

-till next time

# Chapter Four

Aster had stood up and then asked for permission to pick me up to bring me to the kitchen and I nodded my head.

He gently hooked one of his arms under my knee and the other one holding my back and then he brought me to the kitchen and set me down on one of the counter stools.

"I can make you some grilled cheese?" He asked.

"Yes, please." I said with a thankful smile.

Roger and I were supposed to have dinner together so I hadn't eaten since lunch and I was starving.

As Aster turned on the stove and started getting all the ingredients, I looked out the window and my eyes widened when I noticed how much snow had started falling.

"There's so much snow." I mumbled and Aster turned to look.

"I hope it doesn't snow this heavily the whole night." He said and I internally agreed.

As Aster cooked I realized that I would probably have to spend the night here. Or maybe he has a car and he's going to drop me off home? But it was getting really late.

"Hey, do you have a car?" I blurted out and he turned around, coming to sit next to me with the plate of grilled cheese and a glass of what looked like orange juice.

"Yes." He answered setting down the plate and grabbing a sandwich for himself and left the other one for me.

"Will you drop me off at home. Tomorrow?" I asked and he shifted in his seat.

"Hyacinth, why don't you tell me what happened today first." He said instead of answering my question and I frowned.

Oh my god what if he's another psycho and he won't let me go home and keeps me here for the rest of my life?

"You will eventually drop me off right?" I asked nervously.

"Of course I'll bring you back home." Aster said with a hint of amusement in his voice.

"Now tell me, how did this happen?" He said motioning towards my bandaged leg.

"Well..." I started off nervously. "I was on a date with this guy I met a couple of days ago. He seemed really sweet but I was obviously wrong. He was dragging me deeper in the forest and I think he was trying to kidnap me.

I fought him off and managed to run away but I tripped down a hill and hurt my leg against a rock." I summarized and then took a bite out of my sandwich as he stared at me with wide eyes.

"Why do you think he wanted to kidnap you?" Aster asked after snapping out of his initial shock.

"Well." I said after swallowing, "he called someone and said 'I have her'"

"What was his name? Do you have any information on him?" He asked.

"His name is Roger, and he told me he works at the company Les Papillons." I answered.

"Last name?" He asked.

"I actually don't know that." I said biting my lip in embarrassment. I can't believe I went on a date with a man without even knowing his last name.

Carmen was right about being careful.

Carmen!

"Can you get me my phone?" I asked him, remembering it was in my jacket. I realized  that I should tell someone what happened.

"There's no service here." He said and I frowned.

"Internet?" I asked and he shook his head.

"How do you function?" I asked with wide eyes and he shrugged.

"Wait, why do you even live here?" I asked.

"I don't live here. I live in the city but I come down here some-times." He replied. "Mostly during the holidays."

"So what do you do?" I asked.

"I chop wood." He said with a straight face and I stared at him, trying not to laugh.

"You chop wood?" I asked and he rolled his eyes.

"I cook, I relax, I read and I chop wood." He said and I hummed.

Why do I feel like he does so much more here?

We continued to chat as we ate and I slowly found myself relaxing against his presence. After we were done he took the dishes to the sink and I started to feel the need to pee.

"I need to go to the bathroom." I said and Aster came over to my side to pick me up.

He walked to the door near his bedroom and opened to reveal the very clean and spotless bathroom. I realized this whole cabin was extremely tidy and was very grateful for it because I hate staying in dirty places, it freaks me out.

"Be careful and call out to me when you're done." He said, cautiously setting me down on the floor.

"Don't put too much weight on your leg."

"Alright, thank you." I said and he nodded, walking out and closing the door behind him.

I tried my best to not put pressure on my leg but as I stood back up to wash my hands I had to bite the inside of my cheeks from screaming out at the pain.

I hurriedly washed my hands before calling for Aster to come back and relieve me from the pain. He picked me up and sat me down on the couch.

"I think you should sleep on the couch." He said and I shrugged, not minding it.

I hadn't expected him to give up his room for me, after all I was a very unwelcome guest.

"Not that I don't want you to sleep on the bed, but I think you would be much warmer here with the fireplace. There's no heating in my room and it seems like it's going to get very cold from here." He explained and I nodded at him.

"Do you have a spare blanket?" I asked him and he nodded before leaving to go in his room.

He came back with a blanket and two pillows and set them up for me. He watched cautiously as I laid back on the couch and when I had safely managed to do so he draped the blanket over me.

"You okay?" He asked and I hummed with a tired smile.

"Thank you, Aster." I told him and he cleared his throat before mumbling a good night and disappearing in his room.

As I laid there, my thoughts suddenly started slamming into me one by one.

I almost got kidnapped.

I could have died for all I know.

I was laying on a stranger's couch in the middle of a forest.

I wanted to go home.

I sighed with frustration and turned on my side as I tried to clear my head but it wouldn't work.

My throat was closing up as my eyes burned and my heart throbbed with the reminder that I was away from home. Away from my comfort and from the one person who was there for me.

Suddenly, I heard a thump and I sat up on the couch from fright and turned to look at the large window. My breath hitched when I saw a dark shadow and I was gonna scream when I realized it was just a tree.

Now that I was sitting up I became hyper aware of everything around me. The dark room I was in, the crackling sound of the wood burning, the sound of the heavy snow and my own heavy breathing.

The more time that went the more scared I was becoming and I knew there was no way my brain was going to allow me to relax.

I hesitantly placed my feet on the cold hard floor before pushing myself up. I winced at the pain but I sucked it in and slowly walked over to Aster's room.

I raised my hand to knock but then stopped myself. How much more annoying could I get? Already I was invading his vacation time, making him cook for me, making me carry me and now I was going to disturb his sleep?

Just as I was about to turn back around, the door opened itself and revealed Aster.

"I heard the floor squeak, you shouldn't be walking Hyacinth." He said my name in a scolding tone but I could still hear the worry laced behind his words.

"What's wrong?" He asked me.

"I can't sleep." I answered, embarrassedly while looking down and I heard his footsteps approach me.

He grasped my chin with his fingers and then he tilted my head so my eyes would meet his. His grey eyes were soft and gentle and he had a small smile on his face.

"Do you want to sleep here instead, darling?" He asked and I nodded my head.

"Come on then." He said and then bend down to pick me up once again to carry me in his room.

Hello!

Clearly it's not Saturday but I'm making my update schedule random now jsjs.

Thoughts??

This was kinda a boring chapter but I will try the next ones more interesting.

-till next time, whenever that will be

# Chapter Five

Aster carried me in the dark room and I tried to see how it looked like but with my tiredness creeping in and the darkness I could only make out the outline of the curtains and the bed he sat me down on.

As I looked at the bedside table I couldn't help but smile when I saw that he did have a pot of hyacinths. There was a picture frame next to it but I couldn't make out the image.

"I'll get you a hoodie." He said, and moved to his closet and I wondered how he didn't trip over himself.

He came back with a large hoodie and when he handed it to me I couldn't help but internally scream at how soft it was.

I slid it over my head and and wrapped my arms around myself to cuddle it as Aster stared at me. I couldn't tell what kind of expressing he was holding but I hope he wasn't weirded out.

I backed away on the bed until I was at the end and then I flopped down. "Your bed is so comfy."

"Mhmm." Aster hummed as he sat down next to me after draping the large blanket over me.

"Why couldn't you sleep?" He asked softly.

"I don't know..." I mumbled.

"I guess I'm just really overwhelmed with everything that happened and I really want to go home." I said, and then yawned.

"I'm really sorry you had to go through what you did but I promise you, you're safe here." He told me.

"I'm really glad it's you that's here and not someone else." I told him as my eyes fluttered shut.

"And I'm glad that you found me, darling." I heard him whisper as one of his finger brushed a stand of my hair away from my face.

-

When I wake up the next morning the pain in my leg was worse and I wanted to cry.

And it was freezing cold.

I pushed myself up and when I glanced down at the foot of the bed my eyebrows shot up at the wooden crutches sitting there. I grabbed them and hesitantly stood up with them and I'm even more surprised when they're at my perfect height.

It takes a while for me to adjust to it but after a couple of minutes I make it out of the room. When I opened the door I was disappointed to see Aster wasn't on the couch.

I made my way to the kitchen and I found a note on the fridge and I grabbed it.

Good morning, darling.

I woke up a bit early and made the crutches, hope they're good.

There's a spare toothbrush and breakfast in the fridge. I went out for a bit, I'll be back soon.

-Aster

I smiled at the letter and then I opened the fridge to find a bowl of fruits mixed together. I closed it and then crutch my way to the bathroom.

I freshened up and then grabbed the spare toothbrush and vividly brushed my teeth. As I raised my head to glance at the mirror my eyes widened at how messy my hair looked.

I ran my fingers through it and winced at the knots.

When I left the bathroom Aster walked in and he's covered in snow from head to toe and I couldn't help but laugh.

"God, it's so cold." He groaned and shuts the door behind him.

"Thank you so much for the crutches." I said, limping over to him and he smiled when he saw I had no trouble using them.

"I'm glad they were the right size." He said with relief, taking off his hat and jacket.

"What were you doing?" I asked going to the kitchen and grabbing the fruit bowl.

"I was checking the roads. I don't think I'd be able to drive you back today. It's blocked." He said apologetically.

"Oh.." I said, worry taking over me.

I had to stay here?

"Um well there's no one at home that would really freak out and my studio is closed anyway." I mumbled to myself.

"Studio?" Aster asked as he washed his hands with warm water.

"I have an art studio." I answered and his eyebrows raised.

"That's cool."

"Yep."

I sat down on the stool and started eating when I remembered my hair.

"Do you have a hair brush?" I asked him.

"Uhh, I have a comb. Let me bring it." He said and leaves the kitchen.

When he came back I groaned at the small comb he was holding.

"Aster." I said and he winced sheepishly. "This is useless."

"I'm sorry, it works fine for my hair." He said.

I take it and take a small portion of my hair to try and comb it.

"Ow, ow, ow." I cried out as it basically rips through the strands.

"Okay, okay stop." Aster said with panic as he took the comb from me.

"Let me untangle it first and then I'll try to gently comb it, alright?" He suggested and my eyes widen.

"You want to do my hair for me?" I asked and he nodded.

"Come on, finish eating and then we'll go on the couch." He instructed and I agreed.

I finished the bowl and thanked him for the food.

As I moved to take the crutches he stops me and instead picks me up.

"You know you don't have to carry me anymore?"

"It's quicker this way." He said, pulling me closer and my cheeks flush.

He sets me down on the couch and then he sits behind me. "Let me know if it hurts."

His fingers run through my hair first, gently holding each strands and then he slowly untangles all the knots. His touch was so soft that I could barely feel it but then there were moments where the back of his hand would brush against my neck.

"You okay?" He asked softly, his mouth near my ear and I clutch at my hands.

"Yes."

"Wait here." He said and then quickly comes to his room before coming back with a hair tie.

"You have hair ties but not a hair brush?" I asked and he chuckled.

"Hair ties are useful for many things. I didn't think I needed a hair brush when I have a comb."

He settles down behind me once again and then runs the combs through every part of my hair, making sure not the pull to hard.

I thought Aster was gonna do a pony tail or something but when he started parting my hair in different sections my eyes widened.

"You know how to braid hair?" I asked.

"Yeah." He said, his tone changing and I frowned.

I didn't ask why or when he learned and just let him continue in silence.

"There, all done." He said, turning me around and tucking a fallen strand behind my ear.

"Thank you." I smile. "I feel like I've been thanking you so much since yesterday but I'm just really thankful for everything you've been doing."

"Don't worry about it Hyacinth." He said awkwardly and I laughed.

"If you want me to do anything, tell me." I said.

"I just want you to rest and get your leg better so we can take you home, yeah?" He said and I nodded.

Hello!

Thoughts?

Isn't aster just prefect? I mean man can braid hair  And he made her crutches??

-Anyways, till next next time

# Chapter Six

It's been three days since that disaster of a date. Aster and I had fallen into a routine. I'd sleep in his room and he, on the couch. Every morning he would do my hair. Aster said he liked to try new hairstyles and I'd let him do whatever he wanted as long as it looked good.

He would go out for a couple of hours during the day and during that time I would either read or draw in the notebook he gave me.

The snow did not stop falling at all. It just kept coming and coming and Aster told me that the road was even worse then when I first arrived.

I was bored but at the same time this wasn't such a horrible place to spend my Christmas break.

I was warm, comfy, never hungry and I had very good company.

Aster was...

I don't even know how to describe him. Some of the things he did made me doubt if he was an actual man.

All the men in my life were always messing up.

The first man I dated cheated on me after three months of being together.

The second man I dated told me he only dated me because he wanted to sleep with me and after doing so he dumped me.

The third and last man I dated tried to control me and verbally abused me.

I left him.

And of course, Roger, the man actually tried to kidnap me.

Aster, on the other hand, was an absolute angel.

Constantly asking me if I was alright. Giving up his room, clothes and privacy for me. Cooking for me, doing my hair for me and even staying with me until I fell asleep every single night.

He was so kind and respectful that I couldn't help but doubt his actions.

But he never gave me reasons to make him out as a bad person and until he does so he'll stay with the title of an angel in my head.

I was currently in the living room, sketching in my notebook as Aster was out.

I was always wondering what he's been doing but I didn't want to intrude by asking.

As I finished the outline of the fox I was drawing the front door opened and in came Aster, covered in snow once again.

"Hey." He smiled taking off his boots

"Hi." I smiled back, closing my sketchbook.

"You hungry?" He asked and I laughed, throwing my head back.

"Why is that the question you ask me every single time?" I asked.

"Just don't want you getting hungry, now answer me." He said walking over to where I was sitting and flopping down next to me.

"I'm not really hungry, I ate some of the cookies you were hiding in the cupboard." I said with a sheepish smile.

"Mhmm." He hummed, resting his head on the couch and frowning a bit.

"You alright?"

"Just have a headache. I get them a lot." He answered.

"Is there anything I can do?" I asked, scooting closer to him.

"I don't think so." He said.

"Do you want me to massage your head? I know that helps my friend." I offered and he turned to stare at me, his grey eyes boring into me making me shift in my place.

"Are you sure?" He asked and I nodded.

Aster suddenly shifted and laid back down with his head landing on my lap.

"Oh." I laughed, not expecting him to move so quickly but settled my fingers on his temple nonetheless.

He closed his eyes and a gentle smiled appeared on his face as I continued to massage his temple.

I couldn't help but run my eyes over his face.

He had such a beautiful face.

"Huh?" Aster said, opening one of his eyes and my eyes widened.

"What?"

"Did you just say I have a beautiful face?" He asked, his smile widening as heat trailed up to my cheeks.

"Um.. yes?" I replied with an awkward chuckle.

"Do I really?"

"Yes, of course." I said more firmly when I noticed the doubt in his voice.

"You're beautiful, Aster."

It was my turn to grin when I noticed the heat crawling up to his cheeks and even his ears turned red.

"I- thank you?" He answered with a clear of throat and I laughed.

"You're welcome."

I continued to massage his temple, one of my hands trialing into his hair as I rubbed his scalp, my nails gentil scratching it and he hummed in satisfaction.

"Feels so good." He mumbled, sleepily.

After a while I noticed his breathing was getting more even and his body losing the tension.

I continued my massage until I was sure he was asleep and then I grabbed a pillow and hesitantly moved his head from under my thighs and onto the pillow.

When he didn't move, I grabbed my crutches to get the the other end of the couch to grab the blanket and then I covered his body.

I made my way over to the kitchen and I decided to cook for us.

I didn't want him to wake up and start freaking out cause I still didn't eat. He had a habit to becoming like a fussing mother when it comes to food.

I opened the cupboards and smiled when I saw the box of spaghetti.

I took it out, along with all the other ingredients I needed, almost falling down in the process but I managed to do it.

After an hour I was finally done and my stomach grumbled but I decided to wait until Aster was up.

When I heard groaning from the living room I went to check just in time to see Aster sit up, while stretching his limbs.

"Hey, are you feeling better?" I asked.

"A bit." He yawned. "Thank you for the massage, it felt very good."

"No problem, if you get another one and I'm still around then tell me." I told him and he nodded.

"Wait, how long was I asleep? Did you eat? Are you feeling hungry?" He asked with wide eyes, as he stood up.

"Aster." I laughed. "Calm down, I made us dinner."

"You did?" He asked with shock and I nodded.

"Darling, you should be resting." He scolded, walking over to me and I shrieked when he slid his hands underneath my arms and raised me in the air like a toddler.

"Wha-what are you doing?" I asked with a laugh as I grabbed his shoulders for support, my crutches falling to the ground with a loud thud.

"Sitting you down." He said walking over to the couch and gently dropping me on it.

"I'll be back with the food." He said.

He came back after a few minutes with two plates of steaming spaghetti and then he went back to the kitchen to get our juice.

He sat down next to me and I watched with anticipation as he took the first bite. His eyebrows raised and he hummed in appreciation.

"It's very good." He told me and I beamed.

We ate silently and then Aster went to the kitchen with our dishes before plopping down next to me.

"Tell me about you." I said.

"What do you want to know?" He asked and I shrugged.

"Anything."

"Can I-can you like." I frowned at his stuttering, wondering what he wanted to say.

"Can you do that thing you did earlier in my hair." He rushed out as he looked away.

"Oh, yeah sure." I answered, my heart racing as he moved closer to me and laid his head back on my lap.

I settled my hands in his soft, dark hair and he sighed with contentment.

"Okay, so." He started off. "I used to swim in high school."

"Really?"

"Yeah, I was the captain of the swimming team and everything. I really loved it." I could hear the nostalgia in his voice.

"Do you miss it?" I asked.

"Sometimes."

"Hmm what else." He seemed to be in deep thought.

"I love cooking and reading but you already know that. I used to love going for runs back home. I can't draw, but that's okay. Halloween is my favourite holiday. I love Thai food and my favourite colour is green."

"Green? Me too!" I said.

"Really, why?"

"It's partly because I love nature and partly because green is a very calm colour? It represents growth and serenity and I just love using the colour when I'm painting." I explained and when I looked down at him he was already looking at my face, with deep attention.

"What about you?" I asked.

"When I was younger I heard that one of the meanings for the colour green was rebirth and it kinda stuck with me? And I like how it looks."

"Okay now it's your turn." He said. "Tell me about yourself."

I told him how I started loving art, and all my favourite things and he listened with the upmost attention and I couldn't help but appreciate it.

No one likes to talk to someone who can't even pay attention.

We continued to talk as the sun went down and the moon appeared and soon our position changed with me laying back on the couch and his body in between my legs with his head resting on my stomach as I continued to run my hand through his hair.

I didn't know how we had managed to move in such a way but I didn't mind because I was very comfortable and he seemed like he was too.

Hello!

Thoughts?

I just love them sjsj.

I know it's a bit boring right now but I promise it will get interesting soon!

-till next time

# Chapter Seven

The next morning I woke up sprawled on the couch and a heavy weight on my chest. I shifted uncomfortably but the pressure on my body kept me from moving too much.

I blinked open my eyes and when I glanced down my eyes widened when they saw a fluff of dark hair and I realized the weight was Aster.

He was still laying on top of me, his head resting right under my chin and the rest of his body laid between my legs. His arms were tightly winded around my waist and his back moved with the breaths he took.

I had never seen Aster sleep as he always went to sleep after I did and woke up before I did.

Unfortunately I couldn't see his face as it was buried in my-his shirt that I was wearing.

Even after Aster had washed my clothes I was still wearing his as they were so much more comfortable. He didn't seem to mind, in fact he was the one who gave them to me when I went to shower.

I raised my arms and gently started shaking him awake. "Aster, wake up."

"Hmm?" He groaned as he slowly shifted and then he raised his head and rested his chin on my chest. He blinked his eyes open and then they came in contact with mine before he gave me a tired smile. "Morning."

"Good morning." I greeted back, returning his smile.

"Aster." I said when his eyes fluttered closed once again. "I need to go to the bathroom."

That was when he realized where exactly he was sleeping as he immediately pushed himself away from me and sat back on his knees in between my legs.

"Oh god-I'm so sorry Hyacinth." He started off with panic. "I didn't realize I fell asleep on you yesterday. I'm really sorry, I swear I didn't mean to and I-"

"Aster, it's okay!" I giggled at the pure panic on his face as I pushed myself up as well.

"I didn't mind." I smiled at him and the panic washed away as relief shone on his face.

"I'll get your crutches." He said as he stood and hurriedly went to get them from the floor where they had fallen when he had picked me up last night.

He handed them to me and I thanked him before going to the bathroom to freshen up.

When I came back I sat in front of him on my usual spot as he did my hair. I sighed with contentment at the gentle touch of his fingers wracking through my hair.

"Is it okay if I let your hair down today?" He asked and I nodded.

"Thank you, Aster." I smiled over my shoulder and he smiled back.

"You're welcome, darling."

"I'm gonna go freshen up and then I'll make breakfast. I need to go out today and I might come back a bit later but I promise to come back before lunch." He told me.

I desperately wanted to ask him where he was going in such bad weather but I had to hold myself back. I had to respect his privacy and if he wanted to tell me he would.

"Alright, take your time." I told him instead.

-

Aster had been gone for about an hour now and I was immensely bored.

I was in the bedroom reading a book from his collection but I just wasn't getting into it. I sighed, closing it and then my eyes strayed to the bedside table where there was that picture I had seen the day after I arrived here.

In the picture there was Aster and a younger girl, who looked to be about 18 years old with her graduation attire, standing with wide grins on their faces.

I didn't know who she was but she seemed very important to Aster.

She was a gorgeous dark skinned girl with wide curly hair, and she had the most beautiful smile I had ever seen. Aster had his arm wrapped around her shoulder as he smiled proudly at the camera and he looked to be about the same age as he did now if only a year younger.

My first thought would have been that she was his girlfriend but they didn't look like a couple. And if Aster had a girlfriend he really shouldn't be sleeping in my arms or calling me darling.

I looked away from the picture to open the book again and grabbed the glass of juice I had set on the bedside table but because I wasn't looking I accidentally spilled some on my shirt and groaned, hurriedly throwing the book away from me.

I grabbed my crutches and moved to the closet to grab a new shirt. It was the first time I went in the closet myself as Aster had always been the one to grab clothes for me.

I opened it and started looking for a shirt but when my hand came in contact with paper I frowned in confusion and pulled it out.

It was a journal.

I opened the journal and flipped through it, not finding anything interesting until I stopped on one particular article.

21 year old missing girl.

The article said she hadn't come home in five days before it was noticed that she was gone and that's when they went to the cops. I read the date and realized it was about six months ago.

There was a picture of the missing girl, she was blonde with bright green eyes and she was smiling brightly making my heart clench at the thought of her being in danger. I hoped that she had gone back home safe and sound.

I wondered why Aster had this. The only interesting thing in it was that article.

Did he know something about it?

-

When Aster came home I had made up my mind to ask him about it.

I was holding the journal while sitting on a stool in the kitchen when he walked in and greeted me. He asked me if I was hungry and after I nodded he started working on lunch.

"How was your morning?" He asked stirring the pot of the dish he was making.

"Good." I told him nervously.

Why was I so nervous?

"You okay?" He asked with concern and I nodded.

I took a deep breath before raising the journal and setting it on the counter.

His eyes widened in shock and then his face contorted in anger as he snatched the journal away from me.

"Where did you find this?" He asked, and I could hear the anger in his voice and my heart dropped.

I didn't expect him to be angry

"I-I found it in the closet." I answered and he frowned at me.

"Why were you going through my stuff?" He asked, his voice raising just a bit.

"I wasn't!" I exclaimed and he scoffed.

"Then why do you have this? I've been so nice to you Hyacinth and the least you can do is respect my privacy." He told me and I frowned.

"I promise Aster, I wasn't going through your stuff. I dropped juice on my shirt and went to find a new one when I found it." I explained.

He stared at me trying to gauge if I was being honest and when he realized that I was actually wearing a different shirt his face freed itself from the anger it was holding.

"I'm sorry for getting mad." He told me. "I just don't like it when someone goes through my stuff."

"It's okay, I understand." I assured him as the fear of him not believing left me.

"I just wanted to ask about the article about the mi-"

"Hyacinth, don't." He said and by the tone in his voice I decided to shut my mouth.

"I'm sorry." I mumbled.

"Don't say sorry but I don't want to talk about this anymore. Don't worry about it, it doesn't concern you." He said with finality and I nodded my head.

I didn't understand what was the big deal but I wasn't going to say something stupid to make the one person around me angry.

I couldn't afford to have Aster angry at me.

Not when my safety was laying in the palm of his hand.

Hello!

Thoughts?

Why do you guys think Aster got so mad?

Also who do you think is the girl in the picture?

And finally, what do you guys think of the new cover?

-till next time <3

# Chapher Eight

I t has been two days since Aster had gotten upset at me concerning the journal. I didn't bother to ask about it again and decided to forget about it.

Aster was right, it didn't concern me.

My leg had stopped hurting as bad and now I was fine to walk around without my crutches as long as I didn't stay on my feet for too long.

When I woke up this morning and went out in the living room I was surprised to see Aster still sleeping.

What surprised me even more was that he was very uncomfortably sprawled on the couch and his position almost looked painful.

A pang of guilt hits me when I realize it was because of me he was so uncomfortable. I had basically stolen his room.

"Hyacinth?"

I looked up to see Aster sitting up as he stretched his arms.

"Hey, good morning." I smile at him. "You okay?"

"Yeah I'm fine, just my back hurts a bit." He answered and I frowned.

"You don't have to sleep on the couch anymore." I told him.

"Where else would I sleep then?" He asked with a chuckle.

"You-you can sleep on the bed, if you want." I told him, looking away from him.

"But then where would you sleep?" He asked confusedly.

"I mean." I started off. "It's not like we haven't slept together before. I mean- like sleeping next to each other you know? On the couch that day we fell asleep next to each other. So it wouldn't be weird right? Unless you do find it weird-

"Darling." He laughed and I snapped out for my rant.

"I don't mind sleeping with you-I mean next to you." He teased and heat crawled up to my cheeks.

"Right." I cleared my throat and hurriedly walked to the bathroom, slamming the door behind me and ignoring the laughter that left his lips.

-

It was afternoon when I first felt it.

The sharp pain that shot through my stomach.

My eyes widened in panic and I hoped to god this wasn't what I thought it was.

But as the day progressed the cramps were getting worse and I was losing my mind.

I was sitting on the couch clutching a pillow and praying to god to not make it happen.

Aster walked out from the bathroom after his shower and he frowned at the expression I was making, walking in front of me to cup my face and tilt it towards him.

"What's wrong?" He asked.

"You know how you told me you have everything you might possibly need in here?" I asked and he furrowed his brows in confusion.

"Yes?"

"Do you- perhaps have pads? Or tampons?" I asked with a nervous smile and his eyes widened as they too filled with panic.

"You have your period? Now?!" He asked.

"No, it hasn't started yet. I usually get mild cramps two days before so it's gonna come soon." I told him and his shoulders sagged in relief.

"Hyacinth, I don't have pads or tampons. Why would I have that?" He asked.

"What am I gonna do?" I asked him and he bit his lip as he looked away from me.

"It's okay, we still have time to figure it out." He told me as he sat next to me and grabbed my hand.

"What if I start bleeding tomorrow morning?" I asked, not even caring that I'm talking so openly about it.

I never understood why periods were treated as something taboo. It's something normal and we don't have to act like it's a disease or something.

"We'll figure it out, darling." He responded and I scoffed in disbelief.

Just how?

"For now, does it hurt?" He asked with a frown and I shrugged.

"A bit." I said and then I yawned.

"Come on, it's getting late and we should sleep." He said, pulling me up and walking into the room.

I laid down in bed and he got in next to me, leaving a space between us as he draped the blanket over us.

I tried closing my eyes and willing myself to sleep but my mind kept coming up with the worst case scenarios of what could possibly happen.

My period was already bad enough with the horrible pain and now this was going to make it 10 times worse.

"Darling, why aren't you sleeping?" I heard Aster whisper next to me as he turned to his side to face me.

"I can't help but worry." I answered and he sighed, scooting closer to me.

"I promise I will figure it out." He said. "Just close your eyes and try to sleep for now.

I turned on my side and faced him as well.

"Will you tell me something?" I said.

"What do you want to know?" He asked inching closer.

"Anything." I whispered in the dark.

"I... I have a sister." He said.

"You do?"

"Mhmm, she's the one in the picture. She's five years younger than me and she was adopted when she was four and I was nine." He told me and my eyes widened.

"She's beautiful." I told him and he smiled.

"She is. The most beautiful girl in the world." He said and I could hear the pain in his words.

"When I first met her I was angry. I didn't want to have another sibling but when she looked up at me with her innocent eyes and asked me to teach her how the tv worked and I couldn't refuse her. We had been inseparable since.

I was always so protective of her, warding off anyone chasing after her. She's pansexual and she dated anyone as long as they gave her attention and practically everyone at her school wanted to do that for her. It was hard to keep all those horny teenagers away from her.

She was my best friend."

As he spoke my eyes fluttered close and I scooted closer to him until my face was nestled in his chest and his arm fell around my waist.

"She sounds wonderful." I mumbled.

"She was."

-

The next morning I woke up with the pain being worse and I knew it was only a matter of a couple of hours.

When I opened my eyes Aster was gone but I still remembered the feeling of being wrapped in his arms for the whole night.

And then I remembered his last words.

She was.

Was?

I glanced at the picture and I hoped it wasn't what I was thinking. But when Aster had talked about her he seemed so sad, so regretful.

I shook out of my thoughts and left the room to get ready for the day. I decided to take a morning shower and when I left the bathroom in a pair of a new shirt and sweats, Aster still hadn't come back and I frowned.

He's usually back by now.

Another two hours and I was officially starting to worry.

It was so cold out and he must be freezing if he was out for that long.

Just as I was about to go out to yell his name the door of the cabin opened and in came Aster with a plastic bag in hand.

"Where were you?" I asked, rushing to him and when he raised his head to meet my gaze my eyes widened.

His face was all red and his lips were chapped and trembling.

"Oh my god." I said pulling him inside and setting him on the couch before I ran to get the blanket from the bedroom.

I came back just as he took off his hat and jacket and was rubbing his hands together as he blew on them.

I wrapped the blanket around his shoulder and grabbed his hand so I could do it instead.

"Why were you out for so long?" I asked.

"I-I had t-to get them." He stuttered and I frowned.

"Get what?" I asked and he gestured to the plastic bag next to us.

I opened it and I almost dropped it from shock.

Inside the bag was seven packs of pads and four of tampons along with painkillers and a few snacks.

"How? Where did you get that?!" I asked him and he smiled.

"T-the Pharmacy." He answered.

"But it's far from here and you said the roads are blocked!" I exclaimed and he nodded. "They are."

"Please don't tell me you walked." I begged.

"I did." He answered sheepishly. "I promised you I'd figure it out, didn't I?"

"Aster." I said in disbelief.

"Don't I deserve a thank you?" He asked.

I didn't think another second before throwing my arms around him, making him fall back on the couch with an oomph.

"Thank you, thank you, thank you!" I said in his neck and he laughed shakily as he wrapped his arms around my waist and snuggled into me.

"Mhmm you're so warm." He breathed with his cold lips pressed against the crook of my neck making me shiver and tighten my arms around me.

He ran his hand over my back and squeezed me until there was no space left between us at all.

"Can we stay like this for a bit?" He asked, pulling my legs over his making me basically sit on his lap as he buried his face deeper into my neck and messy locks.

"Of course." I mumbled rubbing his back over the blanket.

Hello!

Thoughts?

Aster is literally perfect and I want him.

-till next time <3

# Chapter Nine

Aster was still holding me to his chest as his cold breath fanned the crook of my neck. One of my hands was rubbing his back as the other was buried in his dark hair.

"Aster?" I said trying to pull away from the hug but he tightened his arms around me. "Will you let me go so I can make you some hot chocolate? It'll warm you up."

"But you're warmer." He mumbled and I internally cooed at his adorableness.

"I promise I'll be back soon, yeah?" I said softly and he groaned in disapproval but he let me go.

"You better." He muttered cuddling to his blanket instead.

After grabbing the plastic bag, I hurriedly went to the kitchen clutching at my racing heart.

God.

I couldn't believe what I was feeling. I mean in some way I could because Aster was one of the kindest man I have ever met but still.

Since the moment I met him I had thought he was attractive but now I knew it was more then just an attraction.

I decided to go with saying that I have a crush on him.

I mean who wouldn't, right? It's no big deal. Just a tiny little crush that won't matter once I leave.

But what if it does matter? What if you can't forget him? What if.. something happens?

I ignored my subconscious and assured myself that nothing would happen. After all, I was 100% sure this was a one sided crush.

But then I remembered all the things Aster has been doing for me and I cut myself some slack and went with 80%.

I decided to stop torturing myself with these senseless thoughts and started to make that hot chocolate I promised.

As it was being made I grabbed a box of pads and went to the bathroom. Looking at it made my heart flutter at the thought of all that trouble Asher went through to get it for me.

When I was done I walked back to the kitchen to grab our cups of hot chocolate and then walked to the living room where Aster, despite his large size, had managed to wrap the blanket over him completely.

I stifled a laugh at how funny he looked and set our cups down on the small coffee table.

I let out a small gasp of surprise when Aster grabbed my wrist and pulled me down so I landed on his lap with my back pressed to his front. He wrapped the blanket around me as well before burying his face in my hair.

"Took too long." He whined and I laughed.

"You're being such a baby." I told him as I grabbed his cup and handed it to him before grabbing mine. "Be careful, it's hot."

"Mhmm so good." He said after taking a sip.

"I'm glad you like it." I told him, taking a sip of mine.

"I like everything you do." He said.

"Ah?" I asked with a teasing grin.

"Yep. You're just so... wonderful." He told me and I blushed.

"I think the cold must have gotten to your head." I said and he chuckled.

"I'm saying what I've always thought, darling. When I look at you it's like I can breathe again. You give me hope." He whispered the last part and I furrowed my brows.

"Hope?" I asked and he hummed.

"For what?"

"That's a secret darling." He said stealthily.

-

"Oh my fucking god, please kill me." I groaned rolling in the bed.

"I think that's the first time I heard you curse." Aster mused from where he was sitting next to me.

"I can't." I cried out as another wave of pain hit me.

"Did you take the painkillers?" Aster asking running his hand through my hair and I meekly nodded.

After we had finished drinking our hot chocolate my cramps had started to get worse so I had taken two painkillers. But I knew they wouldn't do much, especially on the first day. I had no choice but to wait for it to pass.

Aster had been the sweetest as usual, staying with me the whole time and checking up on me every few minutes. After he had warmed up he made us lunch and then he carried me to bed where I was now suffering and wishing upon death.

"Aster." I whined as my eyes welled up. "It hurts."

"Shhh." Aster whispered, laying down behind me and pulling me until I was pressed against him. He moved his hand until it landed on my lower stomach and he rubbed it.

"You're okay." He said softly.

"I'm not!" I exclaimed as the tears fell from both pain and frustration.

"I'm sorry, darling." Aster said, wiping away the tears. "I wish there was something I could do to make your pain go away."

"It's not fair." I whimpered and I felt him nod behind me. "It isn't."

"C-can you just continue to rub my stomach?" I asked when I realized it was soothing.

"Of course." He said.

I felt Aster move his hand to slip it under my shirt and then his now warm hand was on my bare skin as he softly rubbed circles.

"Is this okay?" He asked.

"Yeah." I whispered, closing my eyes.

Aster reached his other hand to grab my hand in his own and he gave it a comforting squeeze.

"Is it always like this?" He asked.

"Yeah it's always the first two days that are the worst for me. Tomorrow is probably gonna be worse." I said, already dreading it. "Usually I just lay in bed crying and wait until it goes away."

"You have me now." He told me. "I'll do my best so it's less painful for you."

"Thank you." I said.

Aster pressed me closer to him and then he pressed a gentle kiss to my hair and my eyes widened even more when he brushed my hair aside and pressed another kiss to the back of my neck.

"Just don't want my darling to suffer."

Hello!

Thoughts?

I know this is super short but I didn't know what else to write ('▢ω▢')

Was the second half of the chapter me projecting my own period pain and writing what I wish I had when I'm suffering?

Yes, yes it was.

-till next time <3

# Chapter Ten

My mind was blank as my fingers continued to sketch in my notebook. I let the pencil run over the paper and let myself freely draw whatever that came to me.

I had a habit of doing so.

Drawing or painting without really thinking about what I was going to come up with.

I liked seeing my own creations with a fresh pair of eyes as in I hadn't spent hours staring at the paper or canvas.

When I finally set my pencil down to really look at what I had drawn I did a double take. I blinked to see if I was actually seeing this right.

But even when I rubbed my eyes and looked at the piece of paper the image was still the same.

I drew Aster.

His face that I spent my days staring at or dreaming about was now engraved on this peace of paper.

I was shocked at how I didn't even realize that I was drawing him until I was done because of how detailed his face was.

I ran my finger over it and sighed.

This crush was getting worse by the day.

And honestly it was all Aster's fault. I mean, who told him to be this kind? This sweet and caring?

What kind of girl wouldn't fall for a man who cooked for her, did her hair for her every day and go walk for hours during a snowstorm to get her pads and painkillers?

And on top of that, ever since we started sleeping on the same bed he would cuddle me every night and since that night where I had my period he's been kissing my forehead before I fell asleep.

There was just no way I wouldn't catch feelings.

I decided to dwindle down the 80% to a 73% because of all the affection Aster has been showing me.

I still didn't want to get my hopes high because I didn't know how Aster behaved with everyone else. Maybe he just had a sense of responsibility over me and that's why he was so sweet. It didn't mean he also liked me.

I knew there was nothing I could do about this crush because soon I was going to leave and go back home, back to my normal life.

A life without Aster.

My heart squeezed at the thought and I frowned down at the drawing.

At least I had this to remind me of him. And maybe... maybe once I go back I could paint him instead. Add colour to this colourless drawing.

Aster lived in the city too. Who knows he might want to keep in contact with me once he goes back as well.

I really hoped that would happen.

I want to get to know him more.

"I'm home, darling!" I smiled when I heard Aster's teasing voice and I hid the drawing in the drawer before getting up and going to greet him.

"Did you eat?" He asked as soon as I appeared.

"Yes I did." I told him as I walked closer to him.

"Do you know what tomorrow is?" He asked me as he pulled me down to sit on the couch next to him.

"What?" I asked, glancing down at his fingers as they played with mine.

"It's Christmas Eve." He said and my eyes widened.

"What? Already?" I asked and he nodded.

"Yep." He affirmed.

"I'm really really sorry that you're stuck here with me and not your family." He said with a frown.

"Wouldn't they notice you're gone? Especially during Christmas?" He suddenly asked.

"My parents are probably in Florida or something so no they wouldn't notice unless they called me which they probably will but when I don't answer they'll think 'oh she's probably busy' and call again at New Years." I said with a sigh and he furrowed his eyebrows.

"And you have no one else?" He asked cautiously.

"My best friend Carmen went to visit her grandmother who lives in the countryside side and she's very secluded so she doesn't have any internet and Carmen likes to enjoy those weeks away from the world and just spend time with her grandmother in peace." I told him.

"Does that mean you spend your holidays all by yourself?" He asked and I meekly nodded.

"It's not bad." I said, trying to make it sound better. "During Christmas Eve, I bake myself some cookies and watch a Christmas movie with wine and candles all around my apartment. And the next day I help out in the orphanage and bring the kids food and gifts and spend the day with them painting."

"That's very sweet of you." Aster said with a smile and I smiled back.

"Mhmm, I'll miss them this year." I sighed sadly.

"Well you have me this year." Aster suddenly grinned.

"What?"

"I'm going to make sure you have the best Christmas Ever." He grabbed my hand and pulled me up, making me follow him into our-his room.

"I knew I was spending my holidays here so I brought a lot of stuff with me that my friend, Leo gave me. He said even if I'm alone I should have fun." Aster told me and I realized this is the first time he's told me about someone from his outdoor world apart from his sister.

He sat me down on the bed before opening his closet and reaching for a box on the highest shelf and grabbing. He walked over to me and set the box between us as he opened it.

"Is that a bath bomb?" I said with a laugh when the first thing I saw was a bright pink bath bomb.

"Oh, that idiot." Aster muttered under his breath as his cheeks turned rosy.

"Aww does someone like to take baths with pink bath bombs and bubbles?" I teased and he rolled his eyes.

"It's relaxing, okay!" He defended himself and I laughed louder.

"I know it is, even I use them." I said when I sobered up from my laughter.

"Then why're you laughing at me?" He said.

"I don't know you're just so big I can't imagine you in a bathtub surrounded by bubbles and pink water." I said.

"Well you can see it for yourself later if you'd like." He said and my eyes widened as I stared at him but he just smirked at me.

"W-what?" I stammered and he burst out laughing.

"I'm just kidding, darling." He laughed and I flushed as I grabbed a pillow and chucked it at him.

I ignored the disappointment I felt and I decided to explore the box.

We found ornaments, Santa hats, candles, mistletoes, three ugly sweaters and finally garlands.

"We don't even have a tree." I said holding the fancy ornaments.

"It's fine we don't need one." Aster said as he took out the sweaters.

"Oh god they're worse every year." He groaned.

"Why are there three?" I asked curiously.

"He likes to give me the ugliest ones and make me choose from them." Aster said and I chucked.

"He sounds funny."

"Well now that you're here you can have one. I'm taking this one." He said holding the red one with Santa to his chest as he shoved the other two to me.

One of them was brown with an extremely ugly Rudolph on it and the other one was green with an elf.

"I'll go with the elf one." I said and he nodded, "good choice."

"Why're you so enthusiastic about this?" I asked. "I thought Halloween was your favorite holiday."

"I just want to make sure you have fun. And Christmas is nice when it's spent with the right person." He said.

"And I'm the right person..?" I asked.

"Yes, you're my right person." He said.

"To spend Christmas with." He added after a moment of silence and I laughed softly at him.

Hello!

Thoughts?

I know these chapters are basically all just them hanging out but that is the point for this part of the book. Soon things will change and you guys will most probably miss the simple days jsjs.

-till next time <3

# Chapter Eleven

<hr>

I came out of the bathroom, furiously running the towel over my wet hair and Aster chuckled from where he was sitting on the couch.

"Come here, darling." He motioned with his finger and I walked over to him, sitting on the ground in between his legs.

I handed him the towel which he used to gently dry my hair before he startled untangling the knots with his finger.

"How're you so good at this?" I asked.

"I...I used to do it for Stella, my sister." He said, his voice hoarse.

"Oh." I didn't press much, not wanting to ruin the mood.

After all, it was Christmas Eve.

"There you go." Aster said, patting my head and I tilted it up towards him to smile.

"Thank you."

"You can go shower now." I said and he nodded, getting up and going to the bedroom to get his clothes, I presumed.

He came back out with a pair of grey sweatpants, a towel and the bath bomb in his hand as he threw it in the air before catching it.

"Hyacinth." He said.

"Yes?"

"Will you take me up on that offer yesterday?" He asked and I tilted my head in confusion.

"What offer?"

"To see me surrounded with bubbles and pink water." He told me with a grin and recognition dawned on my face.

"Y-You said you were kidding!" I retorted, aghast.

"I was." He nodded his head. "But I changed my mind"

"I've been doing your hair for awhile now and I would really appreciate it if you helped me out by washing my hair and then you can even see what you've been wanting to see ever since you saw the bath bomb." He teased and my face remained in a dumbfounded expression.

"Only if you want, of course." He said and when I still didn't respond his teasing grin dropped and instead he flushed in embarrassment.

"I'm sorry that was really stupid of me." He rushed out. "I don't know what I was thinking."

And then he disappeared in the bathroom, slamming the door behind him.

Oh my god, what just happened?

Did Aster really just ask me to help him wash his hair while he's in the bath?

I mean.. it's not that weird right?

I slapped my cheeks to wake myself up and then I felt the guilt settle in. God he must have felt so embarrassed.

I gnawed on my bottom lip as I thought of what I should do.

1- Go help him wash his hair and get rid of his embarrassment.

2- Sit here until he comes out and face the unnecessary tension.

I decided to go with option number 1 and so I got up on my shaky legs and walked towards the bathroom door.

"Aster?" I asked as I knocked on it and I heard something fall on the other side making me softly laugh.

"Y-yeah?" He called out shakily.

"May I come in?" I asked and it was quiet for a couple of seconds before I heard his word of affirmation.

I opened the door, surprised to find it unlocked. I tried to control the blush on my face when I saw Aster waist deep in the water. His chest was trickling with water droplets as bubbles surrounded him.

"Is the offer still up?" I asked and Aster smiled before he started laughing.

"God, that was so embarrassing." He said and I laughed along with him.

"It's okay, I'm here now so it worked, yeah?" I said as I pulled the small stool in the corner of the bathroom until it was positioned behind him and I sat down on it.

"Shampoo?" I asked and he hesitated.

"You don't have to do this, darling. Especially if it's because you feel bad for me because of my earlier stunt." Aster said.

"Aster, I seriously don't mind." I assured and after a couple more moments of him hesitating he grabbed the shampoo to give it to me.

"Thank you." He said as I ran my hand through his wet hair.

I opened the bottle and squirted a good amount of the shampoo in my hands before applying it to his soft hair. I massaged his scalp and he groaned in pleasure as he leaned his head back, his eyes closing.

"Feels so good." He mumbled and my face turned crimson at the compliment and at the expression of pleasure he was holding.

He looked like I was doing something else to him-

I shook my head to get rid of those thoughts and continued to thoroughly wash his hair.

"Pass me the shower head?" I asked and he moved forward, grabbing it and handing it to me.

"Make sure your eyes are closed." I said and he nodded.

I shuffled his hair around as I sprayed his head with water and when I was sure all the shampoo was gone I handed it back to him, giving him permission to open his eyes.

He put back the shower head and then he turned towards me, settling his hands on top of the bathtub and resting his chin on them as he gazed at me with his stormy grey eyes. Dark, wet strands of hair fell over his forehead and I reached my hand out to brush it aside.

"Thank you, darling." He smiled and I bit the inside of my cheeks, my heart racing at the adorable expression on his face.

"You're welcome." I whispered.

"Do-do you want me to scrub your back?" I asked and he stared at me, stunned.

"Really?" He asked and I meekly nodded my head.

"If you want- then yeah." I said.

"Of course." He said and turned back around, handing me the loofah and shower gel.

He moved forward so I could have more access to his back and I cautiously set one of my hands on his shoulder and started scrubbing his back with the other.

When I had finished I grabbed the shower head and rinsed his back.

"There, all done." I grinned, satisfied with my work.

He again turned around to face me and then he raised his wet and soapy hand and pinched my cheek making me wince and pull away.

"Ewww you got my face all wet." I whined and he laughed.

I stood up and walked over to the sink, splashing my face with water to get rid of the soap.

"I'll be out, come out when you're done." I told him and he nodded.

-

"We can either make cinnamon rolls or cookies." Aster said as he rummaged through his kitchen cupboards.

After he finished cleaning up he hadn't worn a shirt, which was a first and I had the pleasure to stare at his chest as he moved around.

"Cinnamon rolls!" I exclaimed before a smile took over my face as I recalled the first day I arrived here. "You know some of your shirts smell like cinnamon rolls."

"Yeah I had a perfume that smelled like it and I sprayed it on everything." He chuckled as he took out the ingredients.

Aster started making the dough because I was too nervous to do it, fear of messing up.

When he was done I offered to knead it.

"You need to add more force." Aster said when I tried to do as he said he chuckled and shook his head.

"Not like that-let me show you." He said and I moved to stand aside but he gripped my hips to pull me back in front of it

He got behind me and pressed his cheek against mine, his bare chest pressing against my clothed back and he grabbed my hands to move them in the bowl.

"You need to press harder." He whispered against my ear as he intertwined our fingers together and my mind blanked as a flush crept up my face.

"Like this?" I asked, not even paying attention. My mind was filled with the feeling that his touch and the feel of his breath hitting my neck brought me.

"Mhmm, just like that." He rasped, his voice low.

"O-Okay, I think I got it." I murmured and he turned his head to look at me.

"Your face is so red, darling." He chuckled. "Are you feeling flustered?"

"N-no. You're just really close." I said and he laughed, finally pulling away and went to wash his hands on the sink.

"When you're done, cover it and then we'll continue, yeah?" He said and I nodded, turning my head away and letting my hair fall to cover my face.

God, he was going to be the death of me.

Hello!

Thoughts?

I loved writing this chapter. They're so

I hope you guys enjoyed reading it as much as I loved writing it.

-till next time ♡

# Chapter Twelve

-------------------------------------------------

The next morning when I woke up the spot next to me was cold and I frowned. I sat up in bed and stretched my arms before a smile overtook my face.

It was Christmas!

I slid out of bed and walked out of the room. When I closed the door behind me and looked up my breathing stopped.

Yesterday after we had finished making the cinnamon rolls and devouring them we decorated the house with the limited decorations we had but we had let the ornaments be since we didn't have a Christmas tree.

So then, why was there a decorated Christmas tree next to the fireplace?

I looked at Aster who was sitting on the couch with a grin and a laugh of disbelief bubbled out of me. He was wearing his red Santa sweater and a Santa hat was sitting on top of his hair.

He stood up and walked over to me, gently putting the other Santa hat over my head.

"Merry Christmas, darling." He said leaning down and pressing a small kiss on my forehead.

"Aster." I whispered as tears blurred my vision and my throat clogged up. "H-how did you-?"

"Are you crying?" Aster asked, alarmed and I let out a laugh that sounded more like a sob as I threw my arms around him.

"I-I don't even know what to say." I said, my voice muffled from my face being squished in his neck.

"You can tell me if you like it." Aster told me as he wrapped his arms around me and I could hear the smile in his voice.

"I love it. How did you even get the tree?" I asked pulling away but he kept his arms around me.

"I got it from the forest we're surrounded by." He chuckled as he moved my hair away from my face and cupped it.

"I woke up super early for you and you thank me by crying?" He said as he wiped the corner of my eyes with his thumb.

"These are happy tears." I sniffed and he smiled, moving his face closer to mine until his forehead was resting against mine.

"No one has ever done something as sweet for me as you've been doing for me since the moment I met you and I just I don't know how I'll ever be able to thank you." I told him looking into his eyes as they softened.

"You don't need to thank me Hyacinth. I feel really happy just being with you here, in this cabin. I thought I was going to spend my Christmas alone but then you came stumbling into my life and I couldn't ask for anything else." He confessed and I smiled widely at him.

"I'm really happy I'm spending it with you too." I told him.

"Go freshen up and wear your sweater and then we'll eat breakfast." He said and I nodded, getting out of his hold and walking over to the bathroom.

When I was done I went back to the room to get the sweater and change into it. When I slid it over my head I looked down at the large black sweats I was wearing and frowned.

I looked like an idiot.

I opened Aster's sock's drawer and started looking through it to find some appropriate socks that could replace the warmth of the sweatpants.

When I finally found big white socks that would hopefully come under my knees I took off the sweats and wore them. The sweater was really large so it came to a stop a bit above my knees and so there was only a bit of my legs that were showing.

I decided that I still looked like an idiot but it was definitely less worse than before.

I walked back out and towards the kitchen where Aster had set up the breakfast.

"We had waffles?!" I exclaimed and he laughed at the heartbroken look on my face.

"I was saving them for today." He said.

"All this time." I said with a shake of my head. "I could have been eating food from heaven and you kept it from me."

"Don't be so dramatic, darling. You're having them now aren't you?" He chuckled and I stuck my tongue at him.

I pushed myself on the stool making my sweater ride even higher on my thigh and when I looked up at Aster he was staring at my legs with wide eyes, just now noticing the lack of my pants.

"Aster?" I said and he immediately brought back his eyes to my face where I was teasingly grinning at him.

"Oh-um yes?" He asked.

"Aren't you gonna eat?" I asked with a raised brow and he cleared his throat. "Right."

He sat down and we started eating in silence and then when we were done he took our dishes to the sink and then he walked over to me.

"Stay here, and I'll be back okay?" He asked and I frowned in confusion but nodded my head nonetheless.

After a few minutes he came back with his hands behind his back and a nervous smile on his face.

"What're you hiding?" I asked.

"Shh." He hushed me.

"It's Christmas and the most important part of Christmas is giving gifts. Now clearly I couldn't have gone out and bought you anything but I still wanted to give you something." He said, his voice filled with nervousness.

He brought his hand in front of him and when I looked down my eyes widened at the gold necklace with a small Moon in his hands.

"Stella got this for me on my 20th birthday. She got me two because she didn't know which one I would prefer and I chose the silver one and I've been keeping the gold one with me for as long as I can remember." He said, taking his out from his shirt and I stared at it with awe.

"Aster- I couldn't possibly take this from you. Your sister gave it to you." I said as I stared at him.

"When she gave it to me she said it was because I was the moon to her stars. She said when she looked at me she saw hope, that in her eyes I was always shining bright like the moon." He told me, his voice growing hoarse as he took a deep breath and cleared his throat.

"And when I look at you, darling I feel the same way. You made my dark and empty sky shine with your light. You are my moon."  He said and my breath hitched as my heart started racing at his words.

20%

"So I want you to have this." He said, pushing my hair away from my neck and placing the necklace on it. He moved closer to me and reached behind my head to clasp it and I breathed in his comforting scent as I tried to process his words.

"Aster-thank you. I promise you I will treasure it." I told him, wrapping my arms around his waist while he was still clasping the necklace and he laughed as he hugged me back in the weird position.

"I wish I could give you something" I said with a small frown and he smiled.

"I don't need anything, your presence is enough." He said pulling away.

"Oh!" I suddenly exclaimed when I remembered the drawing I made for him a couple of days ago.

"Stay here, I'll be right back." I said as I jumped from my seat and ran to the room.

I got the small paper out and grinned at it. When I drew it I wasn't sure if I should give it to him since I didn't want to make him uncomfortable but now I was sure he would like it.

When I walked back to go to the kitchen, Aster was walking out and I bumped into him.

"Oh shit." He said, grabbing my shoulders and steadying me before he looked down at the small paper.

"What's this?" He asked as he grabbed it.

"I made it super small so you can fit it in your wallet." I said nervously and when I looked up at him he had an unreadable expression on his face.

"Aster?" I asked nervously.

"You-when did you draw this?" He asked when he looked at me.

"Just-just a couple of days ago. I was looking at the picture and I thought that maybe you'd want to have it with you all the time. It doesn't have colours but I tried to make it as detailed as possible." I told him as I took a small step back but he grabbed my wrist and pulled me closer.

He put the drawing that was a copy of the picture of him and Stella in his pocket and held both of my hands. "I love it."

"Really?" I asked and he nodded, making me smile in relief.

He pulled me closer until we were pressed together and he swayed us in a hug. Suddenly I felt him freeze and when I pulled away I saw him looking up with wide eyes.

I followed his gaze and my expression mimicked his.

The memory of him hanging the mistletoe yesterday flashed in my head and heat crawled to my face when he looked back down at me.

Is he...?

I felt excitement rise to me at the thought and God, I really wanted him to do it.

But I didn't have time to contemplate more because Aster grabbed my face and moved closer until his forehead was touching mine and our nose were pressed together.

Our breaths mingled together as he waited for me to do something and when I slowly moved my hand to cover his cheek, his light stubble scraping the palm of my hand, he got the consent he was looking for and he leaned down, pressing his lips against mine.

The only thought left in my mind was 3%.

Hello!

Thoughts?

Did you expect that?

-till next time

# Chapter Thirteen

----

**M**y hand drifted to the back of his head where I tangled my fingers in his hair as he slowly moved his lips against mine. His lips felt soft pressed against mine and the way he moved them was gentle and sweet, like him.

But then one of his hands that was holding my face cupped the back of my neck and he tilted it upwards as he pressed his tongue against my mouth, pushing and when I parted my lips he slid in.

My heart pounded in my chest as he slowly pushed me back until my back hit a wall and he was pressed against me. As Aster took my lower lip in between his teeth and softly bit a throaty sound left my mouth.

Aster released my lips and he cupped my chin, "Open your eyes, darling."

My eyes fluttered open and when I looked at him he was smiling down at me, his breath heavy and his eyes intense.

"Are you okay? Is this okay?" He asked as he rubbed my lip.

"I-yeah this is more than okay."

"Then can I continue?" He asked and I nodded, my face flaming.

This time when Aster pressed his lips back against mine it was faster and I could feel the heat of his hands as they started to wander. He gripped my hips and pulled me flush against him as I gasped and grabbed his shoulders to steady myself.

He used the opportunity to slide his tongue in my mouth, his tongue meeting mine and he groaned in pleasure as his hand dug into my hips.

My hands stayed rooted on his chest and when I felt myself run out of breath he pulled his lips away from mine. He started trailing kisses from my jaw down to my neck and then one of his hands left my hip to grab the hem of my sweater to pull it aside, revealing my shoulder.

He started sucking on the skin there and I closed my eyes in bliss, arching my back into him.

"You're so sweet." He mumbled as he kissed my neck and then he softly bit.

"Aster!" I gasped in surprise and pleasure and I felt him smile into my skin.

When his mouth started wandering again and he started to pull my sweater down even more I finally pushed him away with my hands that were still resting on his chest.

"W-we should stop." I breathed out and he pulled away from me.

He grabbed my face into his hand and brushed my hair away from it. "As you wish, darling."'

Aster took my hand and pulled me to the living where we sat down and stared at each other.

"So..."I started off awkwardly.

What in the world just happened?

Did Aster just kiss me?

Did I just kiss Aster back?

Does that mean that my crush was mutual?

"So..." He chuckled and I internally groaned.

This was so awkward. What am I supposed to say now?

"Why did you kiss me?" I blurted out.

"Well... the mistletoe and I just wanted to kiss you I guess." He answered.

"So if there wasn't a mistletoe you wouldn't have done it?" I asked as a pang of hurt hit me and his eyes widened.

"No, no! That's not what I meant. I didn't kiss you only because of the mistletoe. If there wasn't one I probably would have done it either way." He rushed out and I breathed a sigh of relief.

Aster grabbed my hand and used the other one to stroke my red cheek making me shift in my position. "I care about you Hyacinth. A lot."

"I care about you too Aster, more than you know." I replied and he smiled.

"And I liked kissing you." He added and I laughed softly. "Me too."

"Does that mean that I'm allowed to kiss you now? Whenever I want?" He asked.

"Mhmm if you want then you have my full consent." I said and he grinned, leaning down and softly pecking my lips.

"Good."

After our conversation Aster had gotten a bottle of wine saying it's the last thing to make our Christmas perfect.

He poured us a glass and we sat together on the floor in front of the fireplace with a blanket wrapped around us.

"Tell me about your art." He asked as he sipped on his glass and I smiled.

"My mom actually wanted me to do ballet like her but I just could never grasp the concept of it. And then I started drawing in this notebook my dad had gotten me and I couldn't put it down. In high school I joined an art club and in college I majored in arts and then my mom gave me her ballet studio which I transformed into my art studio and here I am." I said with a smile as I recalled the days where I would just be in my room drawing for hours.

"That's very cool." Aster said. "I'm a horrible drawer."

"I'm sure you're not that bad." I said with a teasing smile.

"I guess I'll just have to show you one day."

"Guess so." I murmured, my heart racing with the thought of Aster coming with me to my studio and drawing.

"You know." Aster mumbled as he filled his glass again. "I never imagined being here with you."

"Do you wish I never came here?" I asked.

"Well." He started off. "I wish you had never gotten hurt by that piece of shit but I'm really glad you're here with me."

"I'm also happy that I found you. If I didn't I'd be god knows where." I mumbled as I shuddered at the thought of that day.

Aster tensed at my words and he grabbed my hand and pulled it to his mouth, leaving a small kiss on it. "You're here, you're safe. You're with me."

I stared at him as he gripped my hand like he was making sure I was actually here. Was he getting drunk?

"Aster?" I asked.

"Sorry, I just-I don't even want to think about what would have happened if you didn't run away." He said and I smiled softly.

"Well I did. And I don't think I'm ever going to be stupid enough to go on a date with some random person off the street." I chucked.

"Mhm don't go on dates with them." He said and I could have sworn I heard him mutter "or anyone" under his breath.

"Here's to me not getting kidnapped." I said moving my glass to his and he laughed before clinking it against mine.

Hello!

Thoughts?

I'm sorry it's a bit short T-T

-till next time <3

# Chapter Fourteen

Warning: sexual content, if you don't feel comfy with it then I suggest skipping the whole chapter since it's only that

"Aster." I groaned as he sucked on my neck, my legs wrapped around his waist as he held mine in his large hands.

"Fuck, Hyacinth." He breathed out when I ground my hips against his.

I didn't really know how I had found myself in this position but I wasn't complaining.

One second I was getting a cup of water and Aster was behind me leaving small kisses on the back of my neck and the next I was sitting on the counter with him between my legs.

Aster ran his hands over my sides until he reached the hem of my shirt and he raised it, his hands coming in contact with my bare skin and my stomach clenched with need.

As his hand started trailing higher and higher his lips found mine again. He immediately started sucking on my lower lip and when his hand cupped my breast a surprised gasp left my mouth and which he used to his advantage, deepening the kiss.

Aster pulled his mouth away from mine and started dragging it down to my chest and then he grabbed the hem of my shirt and looked into my eyes. When I nodded my head he slowly slid it over my head leaving me bare from the top.

I started to feel embarrassed and remembered how long it had been before I let someone see me this way and started second guessing but then Aster grabbed my face into his hands and looked into my eyes.

"Hey, you're okay, it's just me." He whispered, softly kissing my lips. "We don't have to continue if you don't want to, darling."

"No-I want to, I trust you." I told him and he softly smiled at me.

He let his eyes wander and when they stopped at my chest I swallowed. His eyes were so dark, so deep and they were filled with desire making me flush all over. "Fuck, you're gorgeous."

He started softly kissing my shoulders, trailing his lips lower and lower until his mouth latched onto my nipple making me sigh in pleasure and tilt my head back at the sensational feeling.

His other hand was busy fondling one breast while his mouth continued to pleasure the other one and my hands were pulling at his dark strands.

"Aster-oh god." I moaned loudly when he bit my nipple.

Aster pulled his mouth away and started kissing my stomach going lower and lower until he reached the hem of my shorts. He looked up at my face and asked, "can I?"

"O-okay." I answered as I rested my hands behind my back on the counter and raised my hips, letting him slide off my shorts. I was still wearing his boxers which I was thankful for.

He grabbed my knee and rested it over his shoulder as he started kissing my inner thigh making me bite my lip to conceal any embarrassing sounds that were begging to leave my mouth.

He started nipping my skin with his teeth and my toes curled at the sensation as one of my hands found itself back in his hair. When his mouth started kissing higher and higher my stomach clenched in nervousness.

He pulled away and then he looked at me, his eyes begging. "Can I taste you?"

"W-what?"

"You don't have to say yes and you can tell me to stop anytime." He said. "But I'd really like to make you feel good."

"Okay." I whispered, my face red.

Aster smiled and he stood back up, wrapping his arms around me and I wrapped my legs around his waist as he carried me to his room. "Don't want you to hurt yourself, hm?"

My face flushed at his words and I hid my face in his neck and he shook with laughter.

When he reached his room and closed the door behind him the nervousness was coming back. It wasn't the first time that someone went down on me but the thought of Aster doing it sent a million fluttering butterflies in my stomach.

He gently set me down on the bed and pushed me back until I was laying down. He grabbed a small pillow from the mess of blankets he had dumped earlier on the bed, "Raise your hips, darling."

I did as he said and then he put the pillow under them. Aster was kneeling in between my legs, shirtless but still wearing his sweats since I hadn't dared to touch them when we were kissing.

He leaned down until we were face to face and then he gently kissed me, like he was assuring me that everything was going to be fine. He started kissing down my jaw to my neck, and this time he only left small butterflies kisses on the top of my chest before going lower and lower.

When he reached the hem of my-his boxers I tightly closed my eyes. He grasped the end of it and in one quick movement he pulled them down.

I was immensely glad of the amour of spare razors Aster had in his bathroom because or else I don't think I'd have let him anywhere near me.

"God." He breathed out and I hesitantly opened my eyes to see him looking down at me intensely.

He lowered his head until I could feel his breath fanning against me and I closed my eyes again. He hooked his hands under my knees and pulled them over his shoulders as my heart felt like it was going to explode from the way it was beating.

"You're already wet, sweetheart." I heard him say and I flamed in embarrassment.

I felt his mouth on my inner thigh again and he started kissing all around it. Just when I thought he was finally going to do it he moved his mouth to my other leg.

"Aster." I groaned and I heard him chuckle.

"Yes darling?"

"S-stop teasing and just do it already." I managed to get out and he tsked under his breath.

"I want you to ask Hyacinth. Tell me what you want, nicely."

"A-aster please- please touch me. I need you to touch me." I begged and he hummed in satisfaction.

I hadn't expected him to do it even if I was the one who asked him because when his tongue ran over my slit an incomprehensible sound left my mouth as my hand flew to his hair.

"Oh god." I gasped as he continued to lick me, slowly and gently like he was savouring my taste in his mouth.

He groaned in between licks and the sensation of the sound filled me with pleasure, my hips raising against him.

His hand reached to rest against my lower stomach and then he lowered it until his thumb came in contact with my clit and he started slowly rubbing it.

"Oh god Aster!" I exclaimed and he momentarily pulled his mouth away, his thump still rubbing.

"Does it feel good Hyacinth? Tell me."

"Yes-yes it feels so good. Oh god please don't stop." I begged and his mouth went back to licking me, making me moan.

His other hand reached his mouth and then he used his finger to part my lips and he started thrusting his tongue in me and I bit my lip so hard that I could taste blood to conceal the scream that was going to leave my mouth.

His thumb started moving faster and faster and I started to feel myself getting close but then he stopped and I groaned in distaste.

"Why-why did you stop?" I asked but then his mouth latched on my clit instead and one of his fingers started slowly pushing inside and this time I couldn't conceal the scream that left my lips.

I raised my hips, grinding myself against his face as he started sucking faster and faster and his finger went all the way in.

He took out his finger before plunging it back in making me hiss in surprise. He pulled his mouth from my clit and replaced it with his thumb again as he looked at me.

"You okay?" He asked, his finger starting to move out of me but I grabbed his hand, stopping him.

"No no keep going." I begged and he smiled.

"As you wish."

His thump started stroking my clit in fast movements and this time he added another finger before pushing them inside me.

As he started going faster and faster, his thumb pushing harder against my clit I could feel my orgasm approaching.

"A-aster, I'm going to come, oh god." I whimpered.

"Come for me, darling." He said and then my eyes widened when his mouth went back to my clit without warning.

I screamed as the orgasm came over me without warning, coming all over his mouth and he licked it away, intensifying the pleasure.

When I finally calmed down Aster kissed his way back to me and then he smiled, a wide grin that broke over his face when he saw my flushed face, my hair sticking to my cheeks.

"You were so so good for me." He softly said as he brushed my hair away. "You're so beautiful Hyacinth, so beautiful."

My face turned red at his words and he leaned closer until his lips were pressed against mine. I opened my mouth and let him push his tongue inside and then I realized I could taste myself and I knew he knew too because he was smiling into the kiss.

When he pulled away he laid down to his side and then my eyes widened when I felt his dick press into my hip.

I turned to face him and then I rested my hand on his chest, slowly running it down until it reached his sweats and he stared at me with wide eyes.

"You don't ha-"

I cut him off by palming him through his sweats and he let out a low groan. "A-are you sure?"

"Yes Aster, I want to do this for you." I told him, pressing a kiss against his neck and he closed his eyes as I pushed down his sweats and boxers freeing his erection.

My eyes widened at the size but I tried to conceal my shock by grabbing him in my hand and slowly starting to move up and down making him hiss. He buried his face in my neck and I felt him start to breathe heavily the more I moved my hand.

"Faster." He mumbled into my neck, pressing kisses on the skin and I obeyed.

I started to move my hand faster and faster making him grunt into my neck and move his hips according to my movements.

"God." He groaned when I ran my thumb over his tip and squeezed gently. "That's it-fuck."

I started moving even faster and his groans were getting louder and louder.

"Fuck Hyacinth I'm going to come." He hissed and I kissed the back of his neck since it was the only place I could reach with his head buried in my neck.

"Come." I whispered in his ear and he moaned loudly, coming all over my hand making me smile in satisfaction.

He pushed away from my neck and grabbed my face, bruising my lips with a kiss. "That was so good. So so good. You're amazing."

"I can't believe we just did that." I said with a grin and he smiled back, and after a moment we both started laughing loudly.

Hello!

Thoughts?

I can't believe I just did that oml.

Thank you to  for helping me out!!

-till next time

# Chapter Fifteen

---

A few days passed since Aster and I did....that. Even thinking about it brought a dark flush to my face. I still couldn't believe we had gone that far.

I didn't regret it though. But now I had no idea what was going to happen between us. I had been overthinking so much and I was so tired of it.

But I decided to just go with the flow. I trusted Aster to not hurt me.

Yesterday was New Year's Eve and Aster and I had stayed up until we were sure it was past midnight.

I never imagined starting this Year with feelings as deep as the ones I have for Aster.

But when he grabbed my face and kissed me I knew I was in too deep and there was no way I'd forget him when I go back home.

Aster was out again and I was cleaning up the mess we made last night in the living room while also folding the laundry he had washed.

I walked into the bedroom with the basket and opened the closet to store the clothes inside. As I was doing so I was suddenly reminded of the journal I had found and how badly Aster had reacted to it.

I still didn't understand why.

I bit my lip as I wondered if it was still inside. I reached my hand to where I had seen it but this time I was met with a different kind of paper. I frowned in confusion and pulled it out.

By pulling it out other papers were starting to stick out. I glanced down at the paper and my eyes widened at what I saw.

Amira Misra- Missing since August 2020

What?

Why does Aster have flyers of a missing girl? When I looked at the information it said she was 19 when she disappeared and it's been over a year now since it's currently January 2022.

I grabbed the other papers and I was surprised to see there were other flyers of other missing girls. I shuffled through them but then my eyes widened when I stopped at one in particular.

Stella Reed- Missing since June 2021

The picture of the girl was Aster's sister. She was missing. I swallowed as the pieces slowly pieced together in my head.

Stella went missing and so Aster had all these flyers and that journal. Was he trying to find her? It's been six months now and I knew she could still be out there.

But then I frowned.

Wasn't I about to go missing too? If Roger had kidnapped, me was I just going to be another girl on a missing flyer? Did Aster know what could have happened to me and he decided to act like he knew nothing at all?

The door slamming snapped me out of my thoughts and my heart jumped.

I grabbed the flyers and I left the room with my heart racing. I saw Aster taking off his coat and boots with a deep frown and I chewed on my bottom lip. He already looked upset.

"Aster." I said nervously but he didn't even look at me.

"Not now Hyacinth." He muttered as he walked to the kitchen to get a glass of water and I followed him.

"Aster I need to ask you something." I told him and he finally turned around. When he saw the papers in my head his face paled.

I saw anger flash through his eyes but I could also sense the panic.

"What is this?" I asked, setting down the papers.

"Did you-"

"Yes I did." I cut him. "And I'm sorry but don't you think I deserve to know about this if I was going to be one of them?"

At my words his eyes widened and he set his glass down.

"Well you're not one of them Hyacinth." Aster gritted out. "So now it's none of your business."

"What?" I asked, appalled. "So you did know why Roger was acting shady?"

Aster took a deep breath before opening his mouth. "Yes I did."

"Aster- why didn't you tell me?" I asked.

"Because there was no need to tell you. And now it doesn't concern you anymore! You're here and you're safe. No ones going to be after you so you should just forget what you saw." He said, his voice raising and I took a step back from him.

"I saw Stella-"

"You should leave."

My expression dropped at his words and I stared up at him but he turned his head away.

"W-what do you mean leave?" I whispered.

"Exactly what it sounds like." He said, his voice emotionless. "Your leg is fine, has been fine actually. The roads are also cleared up now and there's no reason for you to stay any longer."

No reason?

"Aster-" but he didn't bother to listen to me as he opened a drawer and dug out keys from there.

He set them down in front of me. "If you walk straight for about 15 minutes you will be out of the forest and you'll see a blue car. Take it and go back home, Hyacinth."

"Do you really want me to leave?" I asked, my throat tight as I clenched the bottom of my shirt.

He finally looked down and met my eyes, his eyes not indicating anything. "You couldn't stay here forever could you? You have to go back home at some point. Just take the keys and go, Hyacinth. Go back to your normal life and forget about what happened here.

"Fine." I murmured. "If you want me to leave then I will."

I walked back to his room with shaky legs as I grabbed the clothes that I wore when I first arrived from his closet.

I removed his clothes from my body and wore mine instead. I didn't even care that the jeans were ripped. I put on socks and I grabbed the drawing I had hidden in his bedside table days ago before blinking back my tears and taking a deep breath.

I walked back out and Aster turned to face me and when he saw me wearing my clothes his face tightened but he didn't say anything.

He was holding my jacket and a scarf of his and I wanted to laugh in disbelief. He was so eager for me to leave.

I grabbed the jacket from him but didn't bother to take his scarf. He could keep his things for himself.

I grabbed the key from the counter but before leaving I stopped.

"Goodbye Aster."

I waited.

I waited for him to pull me back into his arms and apologize and say that he didn't mean it. That he wants me to stay. That he's the reason why I would stay. That he didn't want me to leave him.

But instead he murmured, "goodbye Hyacinth."

I swallowed back the cry that was begging to leave my lips and instead I opened the door and walked out.

As soon as I was outside I was met with the harsh wind of winter and it only made me want to cry more.

But I continued to walk as he instructed. The more I walked the more the pain in my heart grew and I couldn't contain the silent tears that streamed down my face. I bit my lip to stop any sound from coming out as I continued to walk.

But then I heard leaves crunching behind me and I stopped.

Was he.. was he following me?

I fisted my hands in anger and I continued to walk. Even when he was telling me to leave he had the freaking audacity to make sure I made it out of his life safely.

How does he expect me to forget him when he keeps doing things like that?

As I walked I heard his footsteps behind me. His steps matched mine and I wondered if I turned around would I see him?

But I didn't turn around. After all, there was no reason for me to turn towards him.

Finally, I saw the road and I accelerated my pace as I took my last step out of this godforsaken forest.

May I never come back here.

I saw the car Aster was talking about and I walked towards it. But before I opened the door I stopped.

I knew he was still there.

"If you were going to tell me to leave this way then you shouldn't have acted like you cared for me in the first place! You shouldn't have made me fall for you!" I screamed, my voice hoarse with tears and I heard a "fuck" as he backed away.

I got into the car and started it before driving off with a blurry vision.

After I was out of the area I braked and then I screamed as the tears came back with no stopping them. I slammed my head on the steering wheel as I struggled to breathe, only broken sobs leaving my lips. My arm wrapped around my stomach as it lurched.

I never imagined starting this Year with a broken heart caused by the one man I thought was different.

Hello

Thoughts?

My poor Hyacinth.

-till next time <3

# Chapter Sixteen

That first night I came back to my empty apartment, I had cried myself to sleep. I didn't feel relieved that I was finally in my own clothes, in my own bed and in my own home.

Instead, I was missing the comforting scent of cinnamon rolls and the feel of rough fingers softly running through my hair as I fell asleep. I was missing the feel of his lips ghosting against my skin as he whispered hushed words in my ear to make me fall asleep.

The next morning I had finally charged my phone after weeks of not using it and as expected there were two missed calls from my parents and then a Merry Christmas text.

They hadn't bothered to call me for New Years.

I texted them back and apologized for not picking up and then I called Carmen's grandmother's landline.

When I first heard her voice it took everything in me not to burst in tears. I wanted to see her again and to hug her as she would tell me that everything would be okay.

But then she told me her grandmother was getting sick and that she'd have to prolong her trip. I felt selfish for wanting her to come back, because I needed her too but I didn't voice my thoughts out and instead told her to take care of herself and her grandma and that we'd talk when she'll come back.

I felt sad knowing that I was all alone. There was no one I could talk to or no one who could make me feel better about this whole situation.

The sense of security that Aster and the cabin gave me was gone and now I was back to facing the real world.

I dragged myself out of bed. I showered, I wore my comfortable clothes and I went back to my room and sat in front of my canvas and paints I had.

My eyes drifted to the drawing that I had brought with me and then my hand reached to clasp the necklace I didn't give back.

When I look at you, darling, I feel the same way. You made my dark and empty sky shine with your light. You are my moon.

My eyes burned at the reminder of the words he had told me right before kissing me and I scoffed.

How could he do this to me?

I felt anger fill me and I decided the best way to let it out was to paint him before burning the canvas.

And so I did.

I took my paintbrush and I made a copy of the drawing I had drawn of him all those days ago when he was out.

I spent hours painting him. Detailing every part of his face. Making his smile bright. Mixing brown and black to get the perfect shade of his hair. Mixing more paint to get the beautiful shade of grey to paint his eyes.

I didn't move from my spot until I was done. I didn't bother to go eat or take a break. I stayed rooted on my spot until my coloured hands were sore and begging to stop. But I only put down the paint brush when I was done.

I stood up and walked to the bathroom to scrub my hands to wash off the paint and then I finally moved to the kitchen and made myself a bowl of noodles.

I waited until it dried but then I decided it was too late so I had better burn it tomorrow.

The next day I decided I'd burn it after I came back from the studio.

When I came back from work I was too tired so I told myself I'd do it the morning after.

That morning I was worried about being late, especially since I had to go to the elementary school on their first day back from winter break.

When I walked into the school a smile finally climbed on my face at the fact that I'd be seeing the kids again.

I missed them.

I was running through my bag to make sure I didn't forget anything when I suddenly bumped into someone in the school hallways.

"Oh-I'm sorry!" I heard a familiar voice say and my eyes widened in recognition.

Mr. Ross.

Mr. Ross who introduced me to Roger.

He bent down to pick up his file that he dropped and when he stood back up and his eyes clashed with mine they widened in shock.

"M-miss Vernon?" He stuttered and I felt myself take a step back in unease.

Why was he surprised to see me?

"Hello, Mr Ross." I greeted with a small smile, hiding the panic. "It's nice to see you again."

"Yes, you too." He cleared his throat. "The last time I had seen you was during that dinner, yes?"

"Yes." I said with a nod.

"Roger told me he was going to take you on a date... how did it go?" He asked tentatively.

"It didn't happen." I lied, showcasing disappointment on my face and his shoulders relaxed.

"Ah? Why not?" He asked.

"I had to reschedule and by the time I was free I couldn't reach him anymore." I said, hoping he would believe me and he did.

"That's too bad." He murmured and I nervously laughed before excusing myself and hurriedly walking away.

When I walked in the art room I closed the door behind me and clutched at the necklace from habit.

Did he know Roger was a bad man? Is that why he was so surprised to see me here? Did he purposely invite me to that dinner so Roger could try and convince me to go out with him?

My mind went back to the flyers of the missing girls and then I suddenly remembered the words Roger had told me that day.

I'm in charge of getting the toys where they're supposed to be

I have her

Were the toys actually...girls?

Was he the one who kidnapped those other girls?

I decided that as soon as I went home tonight I was going to look up the name of the company that he had told me he worked out before finding that article in the journal Aster had.

-

I sighed as I started walking outside. I regretted leaving my car behind today. After leaving the school I went back to my studio and then I hadn't realized so much time had passed and soon enough it was dark outside.

As I turned the corner of a sidewalk I heard footsteps behind me. I stopped and turned around but there was no one. I shrugged and kept walking but soon enough I could hear them again.

I started walking faster and then I felt thé presence behind me getting closer. I pushed my hands in my pocket and grabbed my keys and just as I was about to run a hand grabbed my shoulder.

I screamed when the person turned me around to face them.

"Wait-wait I'm not gonna hurt you!" He exclaimed and I pushed myself away as I stared at him.

It was a man with a buzzcut and a beard and he seemed to be a bit older than me. His skin was brown and there was no sign of any pimples which made me wonder how he managed to keep his skin so clear and smooth. He had brown eyes and he was wearing a black suit. He raised his hands to his side and I backed away even more.

"Miss Vernon, I swear I'm not going to hurt you." He said softly and I furrowed my brows.

"How-how do you know my name?" I asked, my voice laced with panic as I looked around in hope to find more people on this part of the street.

"Mr Reed asked me to watch over you to make sure you're safe." He said and I just stared at him.

"Who?"

"Um Aster? Aster Reed." He said a bit unsurely and my eyes widened in shock.

"Aster? He asked you to watch over me?" I asked and he nodded.

"But why?" I exclaimed in shock.

"I don't know." He said but I could tell he was lying.

"How do I know you're not lying to me?" I asked and he seemed to think about it before his eyes brightened.

"I have a picture of us." He said and he took out his phone.

He motioned for me to take it from him and after a moment of hesitation I moved closer and grabbed it for him.

Sure enough there was a picture of Aster, this man and another one all standing next to each other with a grin.

"Who-who are you?" I asked as I handed him his phone back.

"My name is Veer, I work under Mr. Reed. We're like an agency?" He said, sounding unsure of himself and I looked at him skeptically.

"If you're going to watch over me then maybe don't follow me as though you're going to kill me!" I finally exclaimed and he gave me a sheepish smile.

I wanted to tell him to get lost. That there was no need to protect me. That Aster should mind his own business. He was the one who made me leave in the first place saying I was safe.

But then I recalled the look in Mr.Ross's eyes when he found out I was still here and the reminder of the missing girls was still fresh in my mind.

And after all, Roger was still out there.

"How did you know it was me?" I asked.

"Um we have a tracker in the car Mr.Reed gave you. It's like that for all the cars from our...agency. And Mr.Reed described you." He told me and I scoffed in disbelief.

A tracker?

"Just walk home with me after work instead of following me like a creep." I told Veer and he nodded, muttering a 'so much for keeping it a secret,' under his breath.

I ignored his comment and we started walking in awkward silence until we stopped in front of my apartment building.

Now I definitely knew that Aster knew a lot more than he let on. I again cursed at my stupidity for not asking him what he did outside of that cabin. Veer didn't sound too confident when he said they worked at an agency and it made me wonder if they did then what kind of agency?

Why had Aster been so dishonest with me? Why didn't he just tell me what the hell was going on? Instead he made me fall for him like a stupid little girl before kicking me out of his life like I meant nothing.

Even while doing so he had the audacity to be caring until the end. And now that I was out of his life he's sending someone to protect me? A freaking bodyguard?

I wasn't stupid enough to throw away the protection though. No matter how much Aster had hurt me or how angry I was I knew there was a reason why he asked Veer to do this.

If he believed that I still needed to be careful then so be it. I knew if Roger showed up again and tried to take me with him there wasn't much I could do.

I looked at Veer from the corner of my eyes and I realized that he didn't make me feel uncomfortable. Maybe it was because he knew Aster or maybe it was because of how awkward he looked.

But looking at him I knew he could protect me. His arms were even bigger then Aster's and he looked like he could kill me with one flick of a finger.

I felt safe knowing I wasn't all alone after all.

We finally reached my apartment building and we just stood there for a moment not knowing what to do when he finally said goodnight and moved to leave.

But before he could I stopped him and dug my hand in my bag, searching for a certain pair of keys.

"Here." I told him as I handed it to them. "Take the car back to Aster."

"Oh-alright." He said with a nod of his head and I bid him goodnight before entering my apartment building.

Hello!

Thoughts?

We all knew Hyacinth isn't gonna burn that painting.

-till next time <3

# Chapter Seventeen

- - - - - - - - - - - - - - - - - - - - - - - - - - - - - - - - - - - - - -

As soon as I entered my apartment I grabbed my laptop and sat down. I looked up the article with the information I had and after searching for a couple of minutes I finally found it. After reading it again I looked up more articles related to it and to my surprise I found two other concerning missing girls.

I then looked up the names of the girls form the missing flyers and sure enough I found them. These girls hadn't made it to the journal and I frowned. I did more research and I ended up finding 15 girls that went missing in the past 3 years.

I bit my lip in thought and wondered if they were all connected. I mean they must be. Does that mean that they're all being taken? Killed? Sold off?

I decided to look up Les Papillons which is the company Roger told me he worked at. Shockingly, the company was founded only 7 years ago. I went on the infringing chart and I found that almost all the workers that were listed were men.

The owner was a 38 year old man named Tage Dawson. He looked normal. But I knew there was definitely more to this. I looked at the locations of their warehouse and when my eyes landed on a specific one they widened.

Previously situated in the forest Bois-Des-Esprits but demolished to be relocated in the city.

Demolished? Did they really? What if they hadn't demolished it. What if the warehouse was still there and that's why Roger brought me there.

What if... what if Aster knew it was there and that's why he was staying in the cabin?

I groaned as my head started pounding with all these thoughts. I felt like the answer was right in front of me but there was still so much confusion.

I sighed and closed my laptop, there was nothing else I could do now.

-

I stepped foot out of my studio, shutting the door behind me and got my phone out to ask if Veer had come.

It's been a few days since I met him and I've come to accept him as a friend. At first I was wary with him following me around but I knew he was only trying to protect me and I couldn't find it in myself to push him away.

No matter how much I tried to deny it, I knew I was terrified.

I didn't want to end up like those other poor girls. Just another face in a missing flyer never to be found again. My heart ached at the thought of those poor girls suffering at the hands of sociopaths.

I texted Veer, asking him where he was and waited for an answer.

Over the last few days we had got to know each other a lot and I was glad that it was him who Aster asked to watch over me and not some other rude person.

We mainly talked about two things; my art whiz he seemed entranced by and his partner. Whenever he mentioned them he would smile fondly and anyone could tell he was in love by looking at him.

He would talk about Rue for as long as he could. Describing every little thing they did and how excited he was to return home to them after work.

Sometimes I felt bad for keeping Veer away from them but he assured me that it was his job and he preferred hanging out with me then reading files and doing actual work.

I also found out that he came to Canada with his mom and younger brother when he was nine. He used to live in India, specially in Mumbai and he tells me he really misses his relatives but he's also really happy to be here.

I had first thought that he was friends with Aster but he told me Aster is more like his boss and that he wouldn't call himself his friend. But he does know that Aster trusts him a lot.

I tried to get more details about what exactly they do but he wouldn't budge on that.

I sighed as I glanced at my phone again and realized he still hadn't answered. I decided to call him but it went straight to voicemail.

I cursed at myself for deciding to ditch my car again. I just hated to drive in the winter and I thought if I had someone to walk home with me I'd be fine.

I put my phone back in my bag and decided to just walk home. It's not like something is actually going to happen.

As I took the familiar path I felt myself relax at the cold breeze. The snow crunched under my booth and with each breath I took it transformed into fog. A flurry of snow started to gently fall and I smiled.

It was dark and the street was deserted by usual but I wasn't bothered by it.

Until I heard light, crunching footsteps behind me. I continued to walk and as I did so they seemed to get closer and closer.

I stopped and turned around but to my surprise the street was still deserted and it was like I couldn't hear anyone.

But when I started walking again they were back, and they were louder.

"Veer?" I called out, hoping it was him again but no one answered.

I was starting to feel dread and my heart was beating extremely fast. My breaths turned shaky as I accelerated in my path.

I was almost there.

But when the footsteps were getting quicker I decided to just run. As soon as I stared running I heard a curse and then the person started running behind me.

I didn't even bother to turn around and see who it was. I kept running as tears filled my eyes and I tried to get my phone out of my bag.

But with the fact that I was running extremely fast I couldn't properly get it and it fell, the loud thud reasoned against the ice and I cried out in disbelief.

I continued to run but the person behind me was faster and soon a hand latched onto my wrist and pulled me in between two bindings.

"Let me go!" I screamed and raised my other hand to hit them but he grabbed it and pushed me against a wall making my bag fall next to us.

I raised my eyes to meet his and the tears fell as I recognized those dark green eyes.

"You're not going to get away this time, doll." Roger sneered and I whimpered.

"Please-Please let me go." I begged as he tightened his hold on my wrists and I felt like I was back in the forest with my back pressed against that tree.

"I quite like hearing you beg but I'll have to refuse." He said and I closed my eyes in disgust.

"HELP!" I screamed and his eyes widened as he let go of one of my wrists to slap his hand against my mouth.

I tried to push away against him with my free hand and my legs but he didn't budge and instead let go of my hand and grabbed a piece of cloth from his pocket.

"No-stop!" I screamed right before he pushed it against my face and forced me to breathe in the weird substance in it.

My protests were muffled and my eyes were fluttering shut against my will and before I knew it, I lost consciousness.

Hello!

Thoughts?

Poor girl can't catch a break

-till next time<3

# Chapter Eighteen

My head was pounding and I whimpered as my eyes slowly fluttered open and adjusted to the bright lighting of the room. I raised my head and when I realized I wasn't in my house memories flashed through my head.

I tried to move my hands but then I realized they were tied behind my back and so were my feet. I could feel the panic swelling in my chest as I looked around.

I was in a large room with dirty grey walls. The room was mostly empty minus the fire extinguisher hanging on the wall and there was a small wood table behind me. On the table there were my coat and boots and when I looked at myself I realized I was only wearing my grey turtleneck, blue jeans and socks.

I tried to think of a way to get out of here when the large door at the front of the room opened and a cold gust of wind entered the room. I realized by the light coming from outdoors that it was now morning.

I had been unconscious the whole night.

I looked at Roger as he walked in the room and when he saw I was awake he smirked and started walking towards me.

"Good morning, doll." He said and I grimaced at him and looked away.

He kneeled down at me and gripped my chin, forcing me to face his disgusting face.

"I expect an answer when I talk to you." He sneered and I blinked at him, not answering.

He chuckled but there was no hint of amusement in his voice, only malice.

"You can act as stubborn as you want but soon you'll be begging and crying for me to let you go and then we'll see who's the cheeky one, yeah?" He said rubbing my lip and it took everything in me not to tell him to get his dirty hands off me.

I could tell my silence was angering him which just pushed me to keep my resolve. I wouldn't give him the pleasure of seeing me break like I did last night, especially knowing he actually liked it.

"Fucking bitch." He hissed as he let go of my face and stood up, taking a deep breath.

His phone suddenly rang and I looked up at him as he walked a few steps away from me and picked it up.

He started talking in a low voice and I could only catch a few words.

She's really back?

The clients-ecstatic to hear it.

Auction- two weeks.

Yes she's not going anywhere this time.

can't wait to see Stella again.

No no she's not going to run away.

My eyes widened when I heard the name Stella. Stella as in Aster's sister? She was still alive? Was she the one who was back?

Roger looked back at me when he heard my breath hitch and then he walked out of the room, closing the door behind him to continue the conversation and I started to move my hands.

I felt hope slam into me when I realized the rope was a bit loose. I looked behind me at the table and when I made sure it was a square table with sharp corners I used my feet to push me backwards towards it.

When I finally felt my hands touch the table leg I somehow managed to push myself until I was sitting on my knees. I backed away until the ropes against the corner of the table and I started pushing it down my hands.

At first it wasn't working at all but after a few more tries I felt the rope slide slower and lower against my wrist until it was around my hands. I was hurrying so much that I didn't realize how hard I was pressing against the corner until I felt it pierce my skin and probably cut it. I bit my lip to conceal the pained groan that almost left my mouth.

I continued to push until finally the rope was around my fingers and then I completely removed it and my hands were free. I immediately started untying the rope around my leg, ignoring the trickle of blood that was dripping down from my hand.

Just as I finished untying myself I heard the door move and I cursed before running towards where the fire extinguisher was. I grabbed it and turned around just as Roger entered the room and saw the empty spot where I was previously sitting.

Before he could even turn around I raised the fire extinguisher with all the force that I had and hit him straight on the back of his head.

"FUCK!" He yelled as he clutched his head and turned to face me. His balance swayed and before he could even try to move towards me I hit him on his head again and he fell on the floor.

I dropped the extinguisher and ran outside, not caring that it was freezing and I didn't even have booths on.

As soon as my socks came in contact with the snow they got wet but I put my focus on running. I ran and ran and then I came to a stop when I was met with a wall of fucking bushes.

I looked around in confusion and when I realized that the whole building was surrounded by bushes I groaned. I didn't have time to stop and think so I pushed myself in the bushes and hoped I would get out of it soon.

I felt the thorns prickle at my shirt and probably rip the fabric but I didn't care. My hair got pulled by them as well and I was sure that I had ripped some of my own strands to get away but it didn't matter to me.

I had to get away.

Finally I felt the bush come to an end and I pushed myself out of it. I continued to run until I was far enough and then I turned around.

I recognized this place.

I was back in the goddamn forest.

When I looked back my eyes widened at the fact that the building... disappeared?

The trees and the bushes hid the building and it was like it wasn't even there in the first place. If I hadn't been inside it a couple moments earlier I wouldn't even have noticed that there was something behind those bushes.

I turned back around and continued to run. I could feel my face freeze and I was probably all red. My feet were going numb because of the cold and my hands were shaking.

I really felt like I was taken back to that day all those weeks ago. But if I managed to get away before then I could do it again.

The more I ran the more I could recognize the place and I felt like I was getting closer to where the cabin was.

Where Aster was

But my feet weren't cooperating with me and soon they gave out under me and I groaned in frustration. My heart was beating erratically and my breathing was heavy and I hated how weak I was.

"No no no." I mumbled as I pushed myself up but my feet weren't moving and my whole body was shivering.

"ASTER." I screamed as tears welled up in my eyes, but I knew there was no use.

Who says he was even still here?

"Aster." I tried once more but there was only silence.

My body was ready to give up and my eyes were closing again as my jeans started getting wet as well and I cried louder.

"A-aster." I whimpered as I clutched at my feet and then I heard rustling and faint voices.

"Aster?" I called louder.

"Hyacinth?!"

Oh my god. He was here. Aster was actually here.

"Aster?" I yelled, pushing myself up.

"Hyacinth! Baby, where are you?" I heard him scream and I started crying even more.

"I-I'm here." I said, my voice hoarse.

"Aster, she's here!" I heard an unfamiliar voice call out and I turned around and I saw him.

Aster's eyes widened when he finally saw me and he ran towards me and I tried to take a step towards him but I was cold and my body didn't have any more strength left.

Just as my legs gave out Aster was in front of me and his arms were wrapping around me and my face was being shoved in a warm chest and a sob left me as I shakily wrapped my arm around him.

"You f-found me." I cried and he pulled away to grab my freezing face and when I blinked I realized that he was crying too.

"I found you, darling." He whispered as he wiped my tears.

Hello!

Thoughts?

I mean...it's not too bad cause she found him right?

-till next time

# Chapter Nineteen

ster slowly pushed me away and took off his jacket, immediately wrapping me in its warmth. My teeth chattered against
each other and I pulled the jacket closer to me as I stuffed my hands
in the pockets.

"Leo, give me your hat." I slowly raised my head to look at the man
besides Aster who took off his hat and handed it to him.

Aster put the hat over my head, covering my red ears and then he
bent down and picked me up. I buried my face in his chest that was
covered by a dark red sweatshirt.

I breathed in his scent that I had missed so much and the comfort
of that came with the cinnamon roll fragrance brought tears of relief
in my eyes.

God, I missed him.

I didn't know how long we walked for, but with the cold taking
over my senses it felt like an eternity.

When I finally heard the sound of a door opening and the nostalgic warmth of the cabin surrounded us I finally blinked my eyes open and pushed my head away from Aster's sweater.

Aster set me down on the couch and then he ran off towards the bathroom. I heard the water start to run and then I faced Leo who was staring at me. Leo was a bit shorter than Aster, with dirty blond hair and light brown eyes. He looked like he was a couple of years older than Aster.

Once he noticed my gaze on him he gave me a smile with an awkward wave. He started moving towards me and then he grabbed the blanket that was set on the couch and draped it over my shoulder.

"T-Thanks." I breathed out as I pulled the blanket closer to me.

Aster walked back out with a bucket of water that he set next to my feet. He grabbed them and gently slid the wet socks off and then he slowly placed my freezing feet in the hot water making me sigh in relief.

"Are you okay?" He asked worriedly as he sat next to me and grabbed my hand in his, rubbing his thumb over the red skin.

"D-does it l-look like I am o-okay?" I asked, my teeth still chattering.

I looked at him and suddenly all the memories came back to my fuzzy mind.

You should leave. There's no reason for you to stay any longer.

I pulled my hand away and pushed it back in his pocket and he frowned. "Hya-"

"No y-you don't get to act like what happened d-didn't. I-I'm grateful t-that you found me and brought m-me here but don't you think y-you owe me an explanation?" I asked my voice hard but the hurt was evidently laced in my words.

"Uh-I'll just go to your room, man." Leo said to Aster and then he rushed to the room, closing the door behind him.

"I'm sorry." Aster mumbled.

"For what?" I asked hoarsely. "For making me fall for you and then throwing me away like nothing we did mattered? For hiding so much from me knowing what could have happened? For lying to me? For kissing me knowing you were never planning to keep me in your life?"

"I didn't-I didn't want to throw you away darling. I wanted-no I still want you in my life. I just wanted to keep you safe." Aster said, his voice begging me to believe him but I scoffed.

"Keep me safe? I got kidnapped a week after you sent me away. You told me I'd be safe. You knew why he was after me all along, didn't you? And yet you didn't t-tell me." I told him as my voice cracked at the end and he winced.

"I'm sorry." He repeated softly

"I don't want your apology, Aster. I just want you to tell me what the fuck is going on!" I exclaimed and his eyes widened at the fact that I swore.

"Okay okay." He said as he raised his hands, as if to touch me but then he thought better of it and dropped his hands at his sides again. "I'll tell you."

"You said Roger worked at Les papillons right?" He asked and I nodded my head.

"The toy company is their disguise. They've actually been doing human trafficking since the company was founded. That day I told you to go home, I had found out that another girl was taken right under my nose. I really thought they weren't after you anymore and I knew you couldn't stay in the forest anymore so I was going to drop you off after talking to you but then everything happened and I just-I got so upset. I wanted to keep you safe but I also wanted to keep you with me.

I regretted sending you off like that but it was too late and I decided to just make sure you were safe. But then Roger got to you again." He said and my eyes widened as the pieces in my head finally fell together.

"You mean... he wanted to sell me? And those girls in the missing flyers have all been victims to this? S-Stella?" I asked and his face tightened as he nodded his head.

"Oh god." I breathed out as bile rose to my throat at the thought of what they did.

"Stella, she's-she's alive." I told him and his head snapped to face me.

"What?" He said.

"I heard Roger on the phone. He said she was back. I heard her name. He said he couldn't wait to see her again." I told him.

"Are you sure?" He asked and I nodded my head.

His head fell down as his body started shaking and I hesitantly put my hand on his back. "Are you okay?"

"She's alive. She's okay, she's okay." He whispered to himself.

Auction-two weeks.

"I-I heard more." I told him and he raised his head, his grey eyes shining with tears.

"What is it?"

"He said something about an auction in two weeks. And clients being ecstatic." I answered and his eyes widened, a flash of anger going through them.

"Two weeks?" He repeated and I nodded.

"Leo!" Aster called out and then his friend walked out of the room. He looked between us before setting his gaze on Aster.

"What happened?" Leo asked and Asher proceeded to tell him what I told him.

"We're so close Leo." Aster told him after he was done.

"Wait." I stopped them. "How do you guys know so much of this? Did you start investigating after Stella?" I asked them.

"We-" Aster started off but Leo cut him off. "Let me explain."

Leo sat down on the coffee table in front of me and then he started talking.

"I've been a cop for five years now. But a year ago there was the first case of a missing girl. I waited for the people I work with to do something. But all they did was search for a bit before giving up. Said something like she ran off with her boyfriend but her family was insistent that she would never do something like that.

I let it go. But then a couple of weeks later it happened again. And again. And yet no one did anything about it. They even stopped publishing articles about it and all that there was were missing flyers. Six months ago I had a fight with my boss and he told me if I wanted to do something about it then I should. He told me to fuck off and stop bothering him.

So I did. I gathered everything we had on the girls and talked to all of their families and eventually I traced it back to the company Les papillons. All the girls were involved with an employee of theirs before they disappeared.

I showed my boss everything and he gave me permission to continue doing what I was doing. I started recruiting new cops that were joining the station and Aster was the first one other than me. He agreed as soon as I told him the situation and soon we gathered enough people that wanted to help us.

We also figured out that the girls were taken here and I knew deep down that they had some kind of base here but we could never find it. I sent Aster here during the holidays to look more closely but we hadn't found it yet."

"I know where it is." I told them and they nodded their heads.

"But it doesn't matter right now. We have to find where they're going to hold the auction and it's not here." Aster said.

"Do you guys know what happened to Veer?" I asked.

"Someone knew he was with you and they called him and told him that Rue, his partner was hurt and at the hospital. When he came to look for you it was too late and he told me and since Leo was already here we started looking for you. We've been looking all night." Aster said as he ran his hand through his hair in frustration.

"Is Rue actually hurt?" I asked in worry.

"No, they're fine." Leo told me.

"What are you guys going to do now?" I asked and they both looked at each other before signing.

"We don't know. We have to find where the auction is going to take place. This may be our best chance to finally catch these bastards and save the girls. We know that many must have already been sold off before but if we catch them this time we could trace the other girls and put the buyers behind bars." Leo said.

"So we need to find out where it's going to take place?" I asked and they nodded in affirmation.

"What if..what if I let myself be kidnapped? For real this time."

Hello!

Thoughts?

Well the cat is out of the bag now.

-till next time <3

# Chapter Twenty

------------------------------------------------------------

"What?" Aster and Leo exclaim at the same time with wide eyes.

"What if I let them take me again? Willingly, this time." I repeat and I know I must sound like I completely lost my mind and who knows maybe I did.

"And why the fuck would you do that?" Aster glowered at me and I flinched, making Leo punch his arm from where he was sitting.

"Aster." He warned and Aster took a deep breath.

"Hyacinth, darling you're not going to let them take you." Aster told me as he grabbed my face and made me face him.

"Aster." I said, pushing his hands off me, making his frown deepen. Since I met him I had never pushed his touch away, instead I was always craving it, craving him. "Let me explain at least."

"If they have a hold of me then surely they would take me to where the auction is going to take place. At the auction they're probably all going to be there and their clients and the girls. They would all be in one place. If you guys have some kind of tracker you can put on or even in me then you could show up the day of the auction and well do your cop thing." I said and Leo's eyes widened, probably realizing that this could actually work.

Aster on the other hand...

"No." He said firmly. "I'm not giving you to them. Are you mad?"

"But this could save all those girls! You could finally catch the sick people who are doing this. You could save Stella." At my last sentence his face hardened and he looked away from me.

"Aster this could actually work, man." Leo said after a moment of silence. "And if we catch them we could trace the other clients who have other girls from previous auctions and maybe we can save them too."

"But you could get hurt." Aster said, turning to look at me again and I felt my heart soften.

"I know." I whispered. "I'm willing to take that risk if it means I could help those poor girls that have been suffering at the hands of those monsters."

"But what if I'm not? What if I don't want to send the only person other than my sister that I care about to the ones who took her from me in the first place?" He softly said and I felt a lump growing in my throat.

"I..." I didn't know what to say at the words that he uttered and I turned to stare at Leo who was intensely looking at Aster.

"I know you care about her and I know you don't want her to get hurt and I don't want that either. I don't want another girl to suffer but this might be our only chance. Our last chance." Leo told Aster.

"Fuck." Aster breathed out under his breath.

"If-if we're going to do this we need to make a solid plan. We need to do everything we can to make sure Hyacinth doesn't get hurt, okay?" Aster said after a few moments of him cursing and groaning to himself and Leo turned to me with a smile of victory that I couldn't return because we had just succeeded in convincing the man I liked to give me up to the enemies.

For the girls Hyacinth. You're doing this for them. They don't deserve this and you can help them.

"I promise Aster I'll try to do my best to make sure she doesn't get hurt." Leo said and I gave him a small thankful smile.

Aster scooted closer to me and when he grabbed my hand this time, I let him. His body seemed to sag in relief that I didn't reject his touch and he moved his free arm to wrap around my waist, his head dropping in the crook of my neck as he took a deep breath to calm himself.

"You know." Leo said, breaking the tense silence. "You're a good person Hyacinth. Not many people would do this. We all say 'if only there was something I could do to help' when we hear of a bad situation but then when the opportunity of actually doing something comes up not many would step up and do it. But you did."

"Ah um thanks?" I said, not really knowing how to reply to what he said.

"Alright so I think for now you two should get some rest and then we can return to the city to think of what we should do!" Leo said and I nodded leaning back against the couch moving Aster with me as he didn't raise his head from where it was now buried in my hair.

Leo got up and walked back in Aster's room and I raised my hand burying it in Aster's hair.

"Are you mad?" Aster whispered.

"About what?" I asked, needing him to specify it.

"About me making you leave that day. About me agreeing to this." He said and I furrowed my brows.

"Why would I be mad about you agreeing to this? I was the one who suggested it." I told him.

"I don't want you to think I want to do this Hyacinth. I don't want you to think that I don't care that you're throwing yourself in danger. Because believe me if I had another choice I would never in a million years send you of all people there." He said and I turned my head to see his face.

His eyes were tightly closed and his jaw was clenched just like his hands that were holding onto me.

"I know you don't want to do this, Aster. If I'm being honest I don't want to either but I'm going to do it anyway." I said and he huffed.

"I hate this." He croaked out. "I hate this so much, darling."

"Me too."

"It's just- it's not fair! Why you? Why her?" He exclaimed.

"I know it isn't. The world is never fair, Aster. But we can make it right. We're going to make it right." I told him and I believed it.

I believed that he's going to do this. He's going to save Stella and all those other girls. He's going to put those monsters behind bars as they deserve and then he can finally be free.

And I'm going to help him do it. I don't care what happens to me while I'm doing it as long as I can help them.

I won't lie and say I'm not scared because I'm freaking terrified that I could cry. But when I think of Stella and all the others who were living their life one day and then ripped from it the next I felt the determination overpower the fear in me.

"I adore you Hyacinth Vernon and I want you to know it." Aster confessed against my neck and then he pressed the gentlest kiss there.

My eyes welled up with tears and I closed them to prevent the wetness from dripping down my face. "I adore you too, Aster."

"Even if I hurt you?" He asked and I could hear the vulnerability in his voice and it made me smile despite the situation we were in.

"Even if you hurt me, and I know you didn't mean to do it. At this point I don't think anything could stop my heart from whispering your name." I confessed and I felt his arms tighten around me.

Hello!

Thoughts?

Sorry for the short chapter

-till next time <3

# Chapter Twenty One

----------------------------------------------------------------

I climbed up the stairs of my apartment complex as Aster followed behind me. I hadn't expected that he would ever get to see my home, my own safe place. It felt weird walking, talking and even seeing Aster somewhere other than his cabin.

I walked down the long hallway until I finally reached the door to my apartment and then I stopped and took a deep breath. I didn't know why I was so nervous of him seeing it.

"Darling?" Aster asked when I didn't make a move to open the door.

"I don't have my keys." I mumbled as I realized I left my jacket back in the warehouse.

Not only did it have my keys but my phone too.

"Oh.. I can pick the lock." Aster said and I moved aside to let him do it but before he could even touch the doorknob the door opened itself and he jumped back, startled.

I moved to see who had opened the door with a racing heart but when I saw my best friend standing in the threshold of my home a gigantic smile broke on my face and I threw my arms around her.

"Carmen." I breathed out. "You're back."

"Christ, Hyacinth." She muttered as she wrapped her arms around me and pulled me closer to her. "I was so worried last night when you didn't come home. I've been calling you all night, where the hell were you?"

I pulled away from her and she started checking me for injuries before she looked behind me and her eyebrows raised in suspicion as she looked at Aster.

"Is that the guy you went on a date with before I left? What was his name again? Rocky?" She mused and I shuddered at his reminder as Aster's jaw clenched.

"No no, that's not Roger." I said with a frantic shake of my head.

"Damn Hyacinth, you already found yourself another man? Why didn't you tell me when I called you!" She grinned as she pulled me inside the house and motioned for Aster to follow which he hesitantly did.

"I have so much to tell you." I told her.

"Dar-um Hyacinth." Aster called out to me and I turned to stare at him. "Can we talk?"

"Alright just give me a second." I told him. "Can you wait in my room?"

I pointed out the door that led to my bedroom and he nodded his head as he walked towards it. Once he shut the door behind him I turned to Carmen with a sheepish smile.

"Hi."

"Hi." She said back with a chuckle and pulled me to sit next to her on the couch.

"Are you okay?" She asked worriedly and I gave her a small smile.

"Depends on what okay means right now." I told her and she frowned.

"Did he hurt you?" She asked. "This guy. Or that Roger guy."

"Aster didn't hurt me." I half lied. I didn't want to explain to her the whole 'leave there's no reason for you to stay' ordeal.

"Roger on the other hand..." I trailed off and her face hardened.

"What happened?" She asked.

"I'll tell you but first let me talk to him." I said and she nodded.

"I hope he knows about your little art project in your bedroom." She smirked at me and I stared at her confusedly before my eyes widened in complete horror.

"Shit."

"Guess not." She laughed at me as I hurried to go to my room.

I opened the door to see Aster sitting at the foot of my bed with his elbow propped on his knee and his head resting against his chin as he stared at the canvas that was standing a few feet away from him.

When I closed the door behind me Aster turned to stare at me with a face filled with awe and wonder. "Is that me?"

"Yes." I mumbled, wringing my hands together.

God this was so so embarrassing.

"When did you draw it?" Aster asked as he approached me and grabbed my chin, tilting my head up to face him.

"When I came back." I answered, peering at him under my lashes.

"I was going to burn it." I added and an amused smile took over his face.

"I guess I did deserve that." He said and I nodded. "Why didn't you."

"I don't know." I answered honestly. "I kept making excuses to myself to prolong the process and before I knew it the painting had been sitting there for over a week and I couldn't bring myself to burn it. I think...I think it was because I didn't want to erase you from my life just yet. My heart wanted to keep you with me even if my mind was screaming at me to let go."

Before I could even start pondering on the fact that what I had said was extremely cheesy Aster had bent down, closing the distance between us by attaching his lips to mine.

I closed my eyes and wrapped my arms around his neck, pressing his body to mine and kissing him back with just as much want as he was giving me.

His arm winded around my waist while his free hand trailed to the back of my neck, tilting my head to deepen the kiss. He started moving and before I knew it my legs hit the bed and I was falling backwards and he was following me.

Just as my head landed on the bed beneath me Aster pulled his lips away from mine and lent his forehead against mine, both of us breathless but wanting for more. One of his feet was still on the ground while his other knee was on the bed next to my hip and his hands were over my head.

"God." Aster gasped. "I missed you so fucking much, darling."

"I-I missed you too." I said as I raised my hand and hesitantly placed it on his jaw.

"There hasn't been a day since you left that I didn't regret what I said to you. I'm always going to regret it and I'm so sorry darling." He told me and I smiled at him.

"It's okay Aster. I forgive you. Just don't do that again, okay? Don't push me away to keep me safe. If you want to keep me safe then just talk to me instead." I told him, my fingers softly rubbing his cheekbone and he nodded.

"I promise I won't hurt you like that again." He said and pressed a gentle kiss against my lips before pulling away.

"You should go back to your friend and then we can talk." He told me.

"Don't tell her too much, okay? I don't want to put another person in danger." He added.

"Okay. I'll try to give her the simple version." I told him and he smiled, leaving another kiss on my chin before pushing himself up and off of me.

"Do you mind if I take a nap? My head is starting to hurt." He asked and I gave him a small smile and nod. "Go ahead."

I sat up on the bed and moved aside so Aster can lie down and he grabbed my other pillow and buried his face in it, taking a deep breath and I couldn't help but smile. I grabbed my comforter and pulled it over his body and then I left a small kiss against his head before leaving the room.

I walked in the kitchen where Carmen was making tea and sat down on the counter stool.

"Everything okay?" She asked and I gave her a nod of assurance. "Everything is fine."

After she finished brewing the tea she poured us two cups and then sat next to me. "Well?"

"Well..." I trailed off and then I told her.

I told her how horrible the date with Roger was and how he turned out to be a lunatic. I told her I ran away from him and found the cabin where Aster was staying. I told her how kind and sweet Aster was with me.

How he made me crutches. How he did my hair every day. How he gently dried it with a towel after my showers. How he always made sure I was never hungry because he was always cooking for me. How he walked through a snowstorm to get me pads and painkillers. How he cuddled with me and massaged my stomach when I was having cramps. How he talked to me every time I couldn't fall asleep. How he made sure I had a good Christmas. How he gave me his moon necklace and told me I was his moon. How he kissed me under the mistletoe. How good and safe he made me feel that day. About every little thing he did for me which made me inevitably fall for him.

A/n: yea this was me trying to convince a few people who haven't forgiven Aster yet to forgive him. (I hope it worked)

"If you don't marry this man I will strangle you." Carmen said as she stared at me with wide eyes after I finished talking about him and I laughed softly.

"He came back with you to the city?" She asked.

"Well...you can say that." I said.

"Now about Roger." Carmen said with a scowl. "Did you try to find him when you came here?"

"Yeah I did. Apparently he left the city." I lied to her because I knew if I didn't she'd hunt him down herself and try to murder him.

I felt bad about lying to her but I knew if I told her the whole story she would never let me do what I intended to do. She would do everything to stop me including tying me up and locking me in her basement.

I will tell her when I come back.

If you make it alive that is.

I shook my head to get rid of the pessimistic voice in my mind and instead asked Carmen about her grandmother.

"I made her come back with me." Carmen said and my eyebrows raised in surprise.

"How did you manage that?"

"She's sick and I wasn't going to let her stay all alone in that small little cottage she has. If she's stubborn then I'm ten times more stubborn." She told me and I chuckled.

"I'll have to go visit her then." I said and Carmen nodded as she stood up and picked up our cups to bring the sink.

"I unfortunately have to go now. I stayed here last night in worry but now that you're safe and home I have to go back to grandma and prepare to open the salon again." Carmen said and my heart dropped.

I followed her to the door but before she could leave I pulled her back and embraced her in a tight hug.

"I love you." I whispered as my eyes burned with unshed tears and I felt her hug me back.

"I love you too Hyacinth." I heard her say in confusion as she tried to pull away from the hug but I held on just a little longer.

I blinked away the tears and finally pulled away to give her a shaky smile and I felt her frown. "Are you sure everything is okay?"

"Yes." I lied and then pushed her out with a laugh.

"Bye!" I yelled and she yelled it back before I closed the door and then lent my head against the door and hoped that I would see her again soon.

Hello!

Thoughts?

-till next time <3

# Chapter Twenty Two

A /n: alright so I know there's no actual tracker you can put inside a human body but in the world of Hyacinth and Aster it exists. (I saw it in a Bollywood movie once and it stuck with me so I decided to include it here)

"You're going to inject this in me?" I asked, pointing at the small chip that was in the tiny case Leo had brought with him.

We were sitting in my living room as early as 7 am because I had work and they wanted to do this before I left. Leo was sitting on the armchair across from us and Aster and I were sitting on the couch with his arm around my waist and his other hand holding mine on my lap.

"Yes. It's going to go on your arm and we'll have to do a small surgery to remove it after." Leo told me and my nerves grew as Aster tensed beside me.

"Are you sure you know how to do it?" Aster asked Leo and Leo nodded. "I've done it before and I'm trained for this, don't worry."

"Alright let's go over the plan again." Leo said.

"Hyacinth you're absolutely sure that this Mr Ross is in on it?" He asked me and I nodded.

"I'm positive. He was the one who introduced Roger and I. When he saw me at the school after the holidays he was surprised to see me, like he was expecting me to be long gone. He looked like he saw a ghost. I'm sure he's the one who told Roger I was back and that's how Roger knew where to find me. If I go back and show up once again after he was sure Roger got me he's most probably going to tell Roger once again." I told them.

"We're going to get him too." Aster glowered and Leo nodded with a clenched jaw.

"Okay so I'm about 90% sure Roger is going to come for you again especially with the fact that you humiliated him by running away twice and not to mention you smacked him on the head with a fire extinguisher." Leo chuckled and I felt Aster smile against my forehead where he pressed a kiss.

"That's my girl." He murmured and I blushed at the words as my stomach flipped.

He had never called me his girl before.

"Gross." Leo muttered as he stared at us and I pushed Aster a bit away from me.

"Okay we can inject this now and then you're off to work. We don't know when it's going to happen but I don't think it will be today." Leo said as he stood up and sat on my other side.

Aster unwrapped his arm from my waist and instead gripped my left hand with both of his.

"Is it going to hurt?" I asked Leo as I rolled up my sleeve and let him grab my arm.

"It might." Leo said as he cleaned around the spot he would inject it.

He got this weird tube thingy and inserted the chip in it before pressing the end of it against my arm.

"Alright, here I go." He said and I clenched my eyes shut as Aster tightened his hold on my hand

I felt a stinging sensation and I winced a bit before it was gone and Leo removed his hands from my arm and exclaimed that it was done.

I opened my eyes and looked down at my arm that Leo was now bandaging and he told me it would be  fine to remove it at the end of the day and that there would be no mark whatsoever.

"Are you okay?" Aster asked as he stroked my cheek.

"I'm okay." I smiled at him and he sighed burying his face in my neck.

"I'm going to go now, good luck Hyacinth." Leo said. "Thank you again for doing this."

"You're welcome." I told him and he gave me another nod and tapped Aster's back before leaving the apartment.

"Are you okay?" I softly asked him and he grunted and shook his head.

"I can't do this Hyacinth." He said and my heart dropped by how sad  he sounded. "I can't-I can't send you to them. I cant watch you disappear from right in front of my eyes. Not you."

"Aster..." I trailed off and I turned my head to cup his face and made him face me. My throat clogged up when I saw his stormy eyes swirling with tears and I leaned in and softly kissed him.

He closed his eyes and cupped my jaw, tilting my head to deepen the kiss and I let the feel of him wash over me as I forgot about everything else.

Because at that moment it was just him and I in  my living room and all I knew was that  I was so irreversibly in love with this man. I loved him more than I've loved anything in my life and all I wanted-all I needed was to come back to him.

I felt tears burn my own eyes and I blinked them open, pulling away from him and instead burying my face in his chest. He wrapped his arms around me and hugged me back and we stayed like that, relishing each other's presence.

"I know this is hard but we can do this." I croaked out in his chest and he sighed. "I know."

"I should go to work now." I mumbled and he nodded, hesitantly pulling away from me.

"Be careful and come back to me. If only for tonight, I want you to come home to me." He told me and I nodded at him, pressing another kiss to his cheek before getting up and leaving him in the empty apartment.

-

That same night I entered the apartment and as soon as the door shut behind me I was being enveloped in large arms as he swayed me from side to side.

"Thank god." He breathed in as he pulled away and grasped my shoulders checking to make sure I wasn't hurt.

"I'm okay Aster." I said and he hugged me again, almost crushing my bones from how tightly he was holding me but I wasn't about to complain.

He pulled away from the hug and pulled me to the kitchen where there was already a plate of steaming spaghetti waiting for me and I felt a smile climb on my face as memories of him cooking for me in the cabin entered my mind.

I freshened up and then sat down as he asked me what happened.

"I did see Mr Ross and this time he didn't look surprised to see me. It was like he knew I managed to get away and was waiting for me to show up. I'm sure he has told Roger by now." I told Aster.

"Do you think...that he's going to come for you tomorrow?" Aster asked.

"I'm not sure. But it's possible." I mumbled and he sighed resting his head against the counter and I continued to eat.

When I finished eating he grabbed my hand and pulled me into the bedroom. I grabbed a shirt and shorts and after doing my night routine and changing my clothes I climbed on the bed next to Aster and he immediately pulled me to his chest.

One of his hands found itself under my shirt rubbing at my bare stomach and the other one was stroking my hair.

"Aster." I whispered in the darkness of my room.

"I lo-"

"Don't." He stopped me abruptly and I looked up at him with hurt swirling in my eyes.

"Don't say it." He told me softly, his thumb still stroking my skin. "Don't say it because you're scared you won't be able to tell me after. I won't let you."

"I want you to tell me when you're back in my arms. Safe and sound." He whispered and kissed my forehead.

"But-"

This time he cut me off by pressing his lips against mine. A breathless sigh left me and I raised my hand to rest it on his cheek as he moved his hand to put it on my back, pushing me closer to him.

He continued to kiss me until I couldn't breathe anymore and then he pulled away and pressed soft, gentle kisses on every inch of my skin that was available to him. We didn't sleep that night, spending the hours whispering hushed words to each other and kissing each other until we couldn't anymore.

In between each kiss I could feel his love for me and he could feel mine. He didn't want us to say it to each other but with the way we kissed, with the way we touched we could hear the words loud and clear.

I love you's that were said without actually being said and instead conveyed through our touch and words filled with promises and hope.

When the sun rose we had a hard time pulling away from each other but somehow we managed and while I got ready he made me breakfast.

We ate in quiet silence as the reality that this might be our last breakfast for a while washed over us. When it was time for me to leave he pulled me to him and I let him hug me for as long as he wanted.

"I'll find you." He swore to me and as he pulled away. "We found each other before and we'll find each other again. I promise you."

That night, I didn't come back home.

Hello!

Thoughts?

Was this chapter weird? I didn't really feel like adding all the details of her going to work and seeing mr Ross so I just skipped it to when she came back. As you can guess the kidnapping happened a lot like it did that night she was taken but again I didn't feel like describing the whole encounter since she didn't really struggle this time and let him take her.

-till next time <3

# Chapter Twenty Three

I, thankfully, wasn't being tortured in a dark room.

Instead, I was simply locked in a dark room for 9 days. The only way I could keep up with the days passing by was because of the fact I received two meals per day.

I hadn't expected this to go the way it was but I couldn't say that I was complaining.

That night, I walked home and I could feel someone following me and as I presumed Roger had grabbed me from the back. I hadn't struggled much and soon enough I was knocked out because of the similar piece of clothing that he had forcefully pushed against my face.

When I woke up I was in an empty and dark room. There was a small bathroom and that was about it. Some guy came and gave me food which consisted of a fruit and water and sometimes (rarely) a sandwich for the second meal.

But now I wasn't in the room anymore.

I had woken up in a moving truck. When I blinked my eyes open I felt panic surge in my chest before realizing that I wasn't the only one here.

I looked around me to see that there were about 15 other girls with me. Some of them looked terrified and others seemed dead.

Not literally, but their expressions were blank and there wasn't an ounce of emotion in their eyes. It was as though all hopes had left them and they decided to stop fighting.

My gaze drifted towards the dark skinned girl that was sitting across from me. Her hair was pushed back and I could clearly see her eyes from where I was. They looked just as dead as the other girls.

Stella.

The brightness I had once seen on her face was gone. She looked like she lost a lot of weight and her shoulders were drooped.

"Stella?" I whispered and her head shot up to stare at me with surprise.

The other girls don't even pay attention to us and the truck continues to roll in silence except from the loud laughter of the men at the other side.

"How-how do you know my name?" She whispered back to me.

"I-I'm friends with Aster. He talked about you all the time." I told her and her eyes brimmed with tears.

"Aster?" She whimpered. "He's okay?"

"He's okay." I told her. "He misses you a lot and I'm sure he'd want to tell you how much he loves you."

"How did you end up here?" She asked but before I could respond the truck came to a stop and the other girls straightened up.

The door of the back of the truck opened and an unfamiliar man motioned for us to come outside. I silently followed behind the girls.

I realized that we were already inside a dark building and as we walked in deeper and deeper I could start to hear voices.

We must be at the auction.

I hoped to god that the tracker worked and Aster and Leo knew that I had moved location and that they were on their way now.

Everything was going according to plan now and I was starting to believe that we could pull this off and soon we'll all be safe.

We finally stopped walking when we reached what seemed to be a back stage of some sort.

"Wait here and wait till your number is called out and then you walk in towards where the arrows are when I call out your number." The man said and all the girls nodded and I did the same.

The man walked away and then after a few minutes we were told to stand in a line. I lost sight of Stella and when I turned around to see if she was there my heart dropped because she wasn't.

I started looking around frantically and when I confirmed that she really wasn't anywhere to be seen I slowly walked backwards and away from the group and when I reached a door I silently opened it and slid out.

I looked around in confusion and hesitantly started walking down a dark hallway. I stopped walking when I heard a muffled voice coming from behind a door a few feet away from me.

I slowly made my way to it and I quietly pushed the door open hoping for it not to make a squeaking noise or else I'd be dead.

I looked in the small gap that I made and my eyes widened at the sight that was in front of me. Roger had one of his arms caging Stella against the wall while his other hand was wrapped around her neck, not in a strangling way but more like he was just holding it.

"God, I missed you babydoll." He said, moving his lips closer to hers and she didn't even try to move away.

I looked down at her fisted hands and the way she closed her eyes in defeat as Roger moved closer to her.

"Hey!" I said as I opened the door more fully.

They both turned to look at me in surprise before Roger glared at me.

"The fuck are you doing here?" He sneered.

"Um-they're calling for Stella. It's her turn." I lied through my teeth and Roger's eyebrow rose.

"Oh?" He chuckled before he turned to look back at Stella and grabbed the back of her head pushing her forward.

"It can't be her turn." Roger said. "She's already been bought."

"What?" I asked.

"Tell your little friend Stell." Roger said.

"He bought me." Stella whispered, her eyes downcast.

"But it hasn't even started." I mumbled and Roger laughed loudly.

"I was supposed to buy her the first time around but the old disgusting shit got to her first. But now that he's dead and she's back she can be mine." Roger said and I just stared at him like he was nuts.

"You know." He said letting go of Stella and walking towards me, making me take a step back but I forgot about the door and my back hit that instead.

"You're not so bad, either." He murmured. "You're an annoying bitch who's persistent in getting away but I remember how good I felt when I finally caught you. I wonder how it'll feel when I break every single ounce of willpower you have."

"W-what do you mean?" I asked with wide eyes and he chuckled, raising his hand and gripping my chin tightly making me wince.

"I mean." He started off. "I should purchase you too. After a bit of time I'm sure you'll come to submit to me and then you can be my little bitch."

"You fucking asshole." I hiss at him and raise my knee, kneeing him between his legs and he lets go of my chin, giving me the opportunity to push him away and run towards Stella.

"Come on, we gotta go." I told her as I grabbed her wrist but she resisted.

"Where are we supposed to go? We can't run away." She told me with wide eyes.

"Yes we can!" I exclaimed and pulled her with me towards the door but then I heard her scream and I turned to see Roger had recovered from the hit and he had grabbed her hair and pulled her back towards him.

"She's mine! You're not going anywhere!" He roared.

"She's not a fucking object!" I yelled at him and he pushed Stella to the ground and started approaching me again.

He put his hand under his shirt and my eyes widened in shock as he took out a gun and raised it at me, pointing straight at my chest.

Before I could even process what was happening, the horrendous sound of a gunshot resonated in the room.

Hello!

Thoughts?

I quite literally hate this chapter but I was tired of being stuck on it so I just updated it. Hopefully the next one will be better.

-till next time <3

# Chapter Twenty Four

----

THIRD POV

Aster glared at the small girl that was sitting on his spot on the couch. This was so unfair! He couldn't believe his parents brought some little girl home and declared that this was his little sister. He was supposed to be the only child. Now his mom is going to love Stella more and his dad will never want to go play with him anymore because he'll be playing with Stella.

So unfair.

"Aster?"

Aster raised his face to face his sister and he tried not to glare too much.

"What?" He grumbled.

"Can-can you show me how the tv works? I really want to watch something." She asked him with her eyes widening and her lips forming into a sad pout.

"Fine." He muttered, grabbing the remote from her and turning it on. "What do you want to watch?"

"I don't know, I've never watched anything before." Stella exclaimed, her dark eyes brimming with excitement.

"Wanna watch spongebob? It's my favorite show!" Aster asked, he too was starting to get excited with the thought of having someone to watch his favorite shows with.

"Okay!" Stella agreed and Aster put it on and then he moved to sit next to her as they watched the song starting.

Maybe having a little sister won't be so bad.

-

"I'll kill her!" Aster growled and Stella grabbed his arm to stop him from launching across the cafeteria table and murdering the girl who was smirking at them.

"Aster stop! You're making it worse." Stella screamed at him, her voice breaking and he turned to stare at her as the tears dropped down her face. He grabbed her wrist and pulled her out of the loud cafeteria to take her to the quiet hallway.

"She outed you little star. She fucking humiliated you, I won't let this go." Aster told her as he held her face in his hands.

"It's my fault! I shouldn't have thought that she would actually be interested in me. I'm a stupid freshman and she's a senior." Stella mumbled as she wiped her face.

"Don't say that Stella. It's not your fault that she's a stupid fucking bitch that cant keep her mouth shut." Aster told her sternly.

"Okay." Stella sniffled and Aster gave her a small smile before leaning down and pressing a kiss against her head.

"Don't worry she'll regret it." Aster promised and Stella groaned.

"What are you going to do?" She asked and Aster smirked.

"Don't you worry about it." At the end of the day Stella was horrified when she heard that her brother egged that girl's car and put her reaction all over social media.

-

"Happy birthday Aster!" Stella cheered as she threw her arms around her big brother and he laughed as he hugged her back.

"Thank you, little star." Aster mumbled into her neck and then she pulled away and pulled him to sit on the couch.

"Here!" She exclaimed, pushing two boxes into his hands.

"This better be good." Aster muttered as he untied the ribbon from the first box.

His eyes widened when he pulled out the small moon necklace.

"A moon?" He mumbled as he traced it.

"Yes, because you're the moon to my stars." Stella said brightly and aster raised his head to look at her with a grin.

"When I look at you Aster, it's like you're shining so brightly, never allowing my light to dim. Whenever I feel lost you're always there bringing me back. You'll always be the moon to my stars and I want you to keep shining, okay?" Stella said and Aster gave her a wobbly smile.

"Little star..." his voice broke and Stella's eyes widened.

"Are you crying?!" She exclaimed and he scoffed as he pushed her away.

"Like I would cry because of a gift you got me!" He said and Stella giggled.

"Awww Aster! You big baby!" She giggled and he glowered at her.

"Shut up." He groaned and then he opened the other box and stared at it with confusion.

"I got you two because I didn't know which one you would prefer." She said. "But now that you have you matching necklaces you can give the other one to your own moon. Someone who's shining for you!"

"As if." Aster laughed. "I'm never telling someone 'you're my mo on.'"

Stella rolled her eyes and punched his arm. "You'll see, one day you'll find that person and you'll give them the necklace and you'll regret ever making fun of me!"

-

"Shh, don't cry." Aster told her as she buried her face in his chest.

"They're gone." Stella sobbed as she clutched at her brother's shirt.

"We're all alone now Aster." Stella whimpered and Aster's own tears fell as he stared at his parents' graves.

"You'll never be alone, little star. We will always be together." Aster swore to her.

"Promise you won't let me be alone?" Stella asked, her voice hoarse from all the crying she had done.

"Promise. It's you and me, little star." He said.

"You and me." Stella repeated.

-

"They're not here!" Aster screamed over the commotion that was happening in the auction rooms.

"Come on Aster, let's go find them." Leo told his best friend and they both left the loud room to find who they had been searching for.

They ran into an empty hallway and then they heard muffled sounds coming from one of the room.

Aster pushed open the door at the same moment that the most terrifying sound he had heard in his life rang out in the room.

"Little star?" He whimpered as he watched his sister push Hyacinth out of the way and her face contorting in pain as she clutched her stomach and fell.

"Fuck!" Leo screamed and Aster was sure he heard another horrified scream. Leo ran into the room and immediately tackled Roger to the ground.

Aster wasn't realizing what was happening. He didn't even know he had moved until he was kneeling next to his sister and moving her into his arms.

"Stella?" He asked and her eyes fluttered open.

"Aster." She whimpered. "You found me."

"Stella please-" his voice broke as a sob left him and he clutched her closer to him with his shaking hands as blood seeped in her clothes.

"Y-you can't leave me Stella." He begged. "I just found you."

"I-I'm sorry." Stella whispered.

"Please-please don't leave me." Aster cried as he pressed his palm against her wound, his hand immediately turning red with the crimson blood that was seeping from the wound.

"I-it's not your fault Aster." Stella managed to get out. "I love you-and it's still y-you and me, okay?"

"No no no." Aster cried as her eyes started closing. "Please don't close your eyes, little star. I need you, please I need you."

"Stella!" He screamed.

His vision blurred as the tears kept falling and his body started heaving with the sobs he was letting out. His words were blubbering words that were incomprehensible to himself but all he knew was that this could not be happening.

"I-I just found you! I'm so so sorry Stella. I should have come sooner. Please don't l-leave me. Please don't go." He begged her, softly shaking her stilled body.

"I love you, little star. P-please don't go." Not realizing that she couldn't hear him.

Not realizing that the person he had been desperately searching for all this time was gone.

And this time it was for good.

Hello!

Thoughts?

PLEASE READ:

So I just want to say that the way I wrote the previous chapter might make you guys blame Hyacinth for Stella but it's really not her fault . The previous chapter wasn't even supposed to go like that but i was in a bug slump and I wrote it that way. It's really not her fault that Stella got shot!!

Stella willingly did it because she wanted to save Hyacinth who she knew was trying to help her and she's also been suffering for so long and her mental health was in a terrible terrible place. She knew what she was doing when she let herself save hyacinth. She just couldn't take it anymore and wanted to be free.

-till next time <3

# Chapter Twenty Five

<hr>

I woke up with a terrified gasp and as I felt my stomach twist with nausea I pushed away the covers from my body and ran to the bathroom.

I kneeled next to the toilet and started heaving. I kept gagging but nothing was coming out since I hadn't eaten anything solid in days. My eyes burned with tears and they started trailing down my face as I clutch my stomach.

When I finally stopped gagging I slowly pushed myself up to my feet and moved towards the sink to wash up. After brushing my teeth and splashing my face with cold water I went back inside my room and sat down on my bed.

I grabbed my phone and the light from it flashed in my dark room and indicated the time.

4:17 am

My eyes drift towards the notification where there was an unread text message from Leo.

hey, just wanted to let you know that we've arrested almost all of the clients who weren't present in the auction and all of the girls are back in their home now. thank you hyacinth, this wouldn't have been possible without you.

take care of yourself, yeah?

I sighed in relief and threw the phone away from me and sinked back down on my bed.

These past few days have been absolute torture. My days are filled with guilt and sorrow and my nights with nightmares and cries of terror.

I couldn't get the image of Aster holding his dying sister in his arms out of my head. I couldn't stop hearing his scream of anguish. I couldn't stop thinking about the absolute pain that was on his face as he cried and held her close to him.

I couldn't help but think that this was all my fault. If I hadn't entered the room then she still would have been alive. She would have been back home with Aster like all the other girls. She would have been safe. But now, Stella is dead and it was all my fault.

It should have been me.

That's all I could think about. That I should have been the one to be shot. After all, the bullet was meant for me. I didn't deserve to be saved like that.

I ruined Aster's life. All this time he was looking for his sister. All this time, his only goal was to have her back. To find her, to save her. And when he finally found her, she was gone again.

I sat back up and moved towards my closet. I grabbed a hoodie and slid it over my body before grabbing my jacket and moving to wear my boots and then I left the house.

As I start walking I think of the funeral.

I hadn't talked to Aster a single time. I couldn't bring myself to look him in the eye after what happened and he hadn't tried to come and find me again so I was sure that he also knew that it was fault.

I couldn't even be sad that he was blaming me because he was right to do so.

When I went to the funeral I had caught a glimpse of him. He was wearing a black suit and his eyes were red, tired and empty. When he gave his eulogy his voice had broken in the middle and then he had left. I didn't see him after that.

I thought back to the conversation I had with one of the girls at the funeral that was at the auction and I sighed.

I hugged back the girl who was currently weeping in my neck and when she pulled away she apologized and wiped her face.

"I-I'm sorry, I'm just so thankful for what you did for us." She sniffled and I gave her a small smile.

"I didn't do anything." I told her but she shook her head.

"No, I know you did. If it weren't for you then we would have still been in that hell." She said.

"I want you to know that you don't have to feel guilty." She softly said and my eyes widened as I stared at her.

"When Stella came back from her old client I had stumbled upon her one day. She was..she was trying to kill herself. I stopped her and

I told her that she couldn't give up and give them that kind of power over her but she was hysterical saying that she couldn't do it anymore. I didn't understand  at first but then she told me what happened to her with that client.

And I couldn't...I couldn't even begin to imagine how that must have been for her. She spent 4 months with that.. monster. Even I, who hasn't even been through half of what she did, would have made the same decision she did. I know that she would have done it all over again if she could, so I'm telling you, it's not your fault she died." The young girl told me and my lips wobbled as my eyes filled with tears.

"I-I'm sorry I need-I need to go. Thank you for saying this." I told her and then I turned around and left with my heart shattered.

Despite what she told me there was still an unbearable guilt in me and I knew that it would never go away.

When I finally reached my destination the sun was starting to rise. I pushed open the gate and winced at the squeaking sound it made.

I slowly walked towards where I knew Stella was but then I stopped when I saw a body hunched up in front of the grave. I was ready to turn back around and leave but then he turned around and my eyes clashed with his stormy ones.

My throat closed up as my eyes run over him. His eyes were heavy with lack of sleep and I could see the dark circles from where I was standing. His hair was tousled and his faint stubble had grown a lot.

"Hyacinth." He breathed out and I took a step back.

"I-I'm sorry, I didn't mean to interrupt you. I'll leave." I said and was about to turn around to do so but then his voice reached my ears again and I stopped.

"Don't go." He whispered.

"Y-You don't want me to leave?" I asked and he shook his head.

"I want you to come here." He said and I hesitantly walked towards him.

He reached his hand for me and I grabbed it and then a surprised sound left me when he pulled me down towards him and into his arms.

"I'm sorry." He whispered in my neck and I furrowed my brows

"Why are you apologizing? I should be the one to apologize." I told him, my voice slightly mumble from where my face was pressed against his chest.

"Because I haven't talked to you. I've just been.. so in my head that I couldn't bring myself to do anything. I'm sorry for not reaching out to you. How are you?" He asked softly as he pulled away from the hug and cupped my face.

"Aster." I whispered in disbelief. "How-how are you okay to talk to me? I-I did this Aster, it should have been me. You should hate me."

"What?" He asked with wide eyes.

"Hyacinth-no. It's not your fault, baby." He said and then he wiped the corner of my eye where a traitorous tear had appeared.

"I'm sorry." I whimpered, looking down in my lap.

"Look at me, darling." Aster ordered firmly and I did as he asked of me.

"I already lost the one person I loved the most in the world." He said hoarsely and I closed my eyes as the guilty was surely to appear in them.

"I don't want to lose the other."

At his words my eyes shot open and I stared at him in shock.

"What..?" I breathed out.

"I love you." He softly murmured as his thump stroked my cheek. "I love you so much and I'm so glad to know you're safe. That you're still here with me. I don't know what I would have done if something happened to you too."

"Aster." I cried and buried my face in his chest and as he wrapped his arms around me and pulled me closer.

"I love you too." I told him and his arms tightened around me. "And I'm so sorry that you lost her."

"I know." He mumbled, kissing my head.

"She loved you so much, Aster. I'm sure she was happy that she got to see you. You did everything you could to save her and she knows that." I told him, pulling away and he took a deep shuddering breath.

"I miss her." He softly whispered.

"I know." I said softly, cupping his face and he leaned in the touch.

"I miss her so much, Hyacinth. How-how am I supposed to go on like this? It was always her and I and now she's gone and I'm still here and I just-I just don't know how to live in a world where my little star isn't with me." He said and my heart twisted with pain at the sight of him in this much pain.

"She'll always be with you." I told him as my fingers found the necklace around his neck. "She'll always be with you, Aster. And she'll want you to keep shining brightly for her so she can watch over you, yeah?"

"She needs her moon to keep shining, Aster. Don't let your light die." I said and a quiet sob left his lips as he covered his face.

"I just miss her so much." He cried and I wrapped my arms around him, pulling him closer to me and let him wept in my chest.

"I know, baby, I know." I murmured to him as he continued to cry.

"Do-do you think she was happy in her last moments? I didn't want her to be sad. I wanted her to know that I loved her. But she didn't-she didn't hear." He whimpered as he pulled away.

"I told her you loved her when I saw her. She knows how much you love her, okay?" I told him stroking his hair and he hummed.

"You did?" He asked.

"I did." I told him and he gave me a small smile.

"I love you so much." He mumbled.

"I love you, Aster." I replied and leaned closer to leave a kiss against his jaw.

# Epilogue

Six months later~

My hand delicately held the paintbrush and I continued to brush it over the now very colourful canvas that was in front of me. I started this piece months ago and I've been working on it for so long.

I was taking so much time since I wanted it to be perfect and also because I was hiding it from Aster. I could only work on it when he wasn't with me and nowadays that left me with little time.

Not that I minded.

Aster has been taking me out on so many dates and giving me practically everything I asked for and I couldn't believe how sweet and perfect that man was.

Sometimes he had moments of weaknesses where he would break down and try to push me away but I never let him. I gave him the space he needed but I always made sure he knew I was right there for him.

It was very hard for the both of us to come to terms with what happened and we both had nightmares for quite awhile but Aster had started seeing someone to help with his insomnia and night terrors since they were much worse then the ones I had.

Talking about everything that happened has helped him cope and he started going to the gym with Leo quite frequently and that also helped him lose some tension.

When I woke up from nightmares Aster would usually already be awake and he would hush me back to sleep while whispering sweet nothings in my ear.

The only things that kept me distracted enough to forget about everything we went through were Aster and painting.

And I've been giving all my time to both of them and I finally feel happy. Genuinely happy.

Currently Aster was at work and he was coming over for dinner where I planned to give him the painting and talk to him about what I've been thinking about for weeks.

I shook myself out of my thoughts and continued finishing up on the details of the painting. Just as I did the final brush the doorbell rang and I hurriedly stood up to wash my hands before opening the door.

"Hi, darling." Aster grinned at me as he leaned down and pecked my lip.

"Hi." I smiled at him. "Come on in, I just need to heat up the food and we can eat."

"Alright, I'm going to go wash up real quick." He said and I nodded as he walked towards the bathroom and I to the kitchen.

I took out two servings of the fried rice I made and after hearing them up I set them on my dining table and decided to grab the bottle of wine I had been saving for a special occasion.

"Wine?" Aster asked as he walked inside and took the seat across from me.

"Yeah, I thought we could drink and enjoy today since there's no work for both of us tomorrow." I told him and he smirked.

"Enjoy, you say?" He grinned cheekily and I rolled my eyes despite the blush climbing on my face.

"Shut up and eat." I muttered and then took a spoonful of the rice.

He laughed quietly but started eating as I told him to. We continued to eat in a comforting silence and as our dinner came closer to an end I started fidgeting in my spot in nervousness and he seemed to notice.

"Are you alright?" He asked and I nodded.

"Yes I'm fine." I told him.

"I just wanted to talk to you about something." I said.

"Do you want to go to the living room to talk?" He asked and I nodded my head as we both got up and moved to sit on the couch.

His arm looped around my waist and I instinctively leaned my head on his shoulder.

"So I know you've been staying with Leo to save money for when you get a new apartment soon." I started off and I saw his expression shift as he realized where this conversation was going.

"My apartment lease is ending in a few weeks and I was just think-ing that we could...you know move in together? Search for an apart-ment together and all. I mean you're already sleeping over here most nights anyways." I nervously started ranting. "But you don't have to if you don't want to. I mean it is kinda early and-"

Aster cut me off by cupping the back of my neck and pressing his lips against mine. I felt myself relax and I closed my eyes while kissing him back.

"Yes." He breathed out after breaking the kiss and I gave him a big smile that he reciprocated. "I was actually going to talk to you about the same thing."

"Really?" I asked and he nodded his head.

"We should start searching for apartments tomorrow!" I exclaimed with excitement and Aster chuckled fondly.

I buried my face in his chest and he wrapped both arms around me in a tight hug and I breathed in his cinnamon roll.

"I'm so happy." I mumbled and I felt him rub my back. "Me too, darling, me too."

"I have something for you." I told Aster and stood up, grabbing his arm and leading him in the bedroom.

"Oh?" He asked and I could practically see the smirk that was most probably on his face.

"Is sex all you ever think about?" I asked incredulously and he laughed loudly.

"You're the one who said it, not me." He said and I blushed.

"I can't believe you." I muttered but there was a smile on my face nonetheless.

"Close your eyes." I told him and he did as I asked as I led him to sit on the bed.

I moved the painting closer to him and then I told him to open his eyes. I watched as the expression on his face changed from curiosity, to shock, to awe and finally to disbelief.

"Is this...?" He asked and I nodded nervously.

I turned to look at the painting too and couldn't help but feel proud at it along with nervousness that maybe I shouldn't have. It was a painting of a young girl and a young boy standing on the moon surrounded by bright light and then stars all around them.

"Hyacinth..." Aster whispered, his voice rough and when I turned to look at him again I felt panic grown in me because of the tears in his eyes.

"Oh god." I said as I approached him and immediately wrapped him in a hug, his face nestling on my stomach as he wrapped his arms tightly around my back.

"I'm sorry, Aster. I didn't mean to make you cry. I'm sorry." I mumbled, running my fingers through his hair.

"Don't say sorry." He said. "I love it so much."

"You do?" I asked hopefully and I felt him nod before he pulled away from the hug only to grip the back of my thighs and push me forward until I landed on his lap, my legs straddling him.

"I love it and I love you." He murmured as he pressed butterfly kisses all over my face.

"I love you Aster. So much." I replied with a smile on my face.

The end.